# THE
# PURGING ROOM

*A Novella*

RANDY ELROD

*First Edition*

ISBN: 978-0-9914715-9-1

www.randyelrod.com

Printed in the United States of America

This is a work of fiction. While certain characters share names and general philosophical concepts with historical figures, their portrayals, dialogue, personal anecdotes, and the encounters depicted herein are products of the author's imagination. Any resemblance to actual persons, living or dead, or actual events is purely coincidental. References to published works are for creative purposes only and do not represent the actual content or endorsement of those works or their authors.

Cover design by Noah at 99Designs

For those who have dared to walk through transformative doorways and for those still searching for them.

# Table of Contents

# CHAPTER ONE

## Manhattan Arrival

They say God speaks in whispers, but all I heard as our jet descended into New York was silence—the kind that happens when you've spent decades denying your voice. Stepping off the plane from Shanghai, I realized yet again that success has a distinctive scent—antiseptic, metallic, and utterly devoid of joy.

The problem with the American dream, he thought, as Manhattan's skyline came into view through the taxi window, was that it had delivered him exactly to where he'd aimed and nowhere near where he belonged. The desolate emptiness that comes with achieving everything he'd bled for settled into his bones as the taxi pulled up to The Plaza Hotel.

oooo

After checking into his favorite room, the Terrace Suite, he freshened up, opened the doors to the expansive balcony, walked to the edge, and surveyed Central Park from the top floor. It was March 20, 2002, Spring Equinox, but a chilly wind sent shivers down his spine. The 30-degree weather was a stark contrast to the 60s in Shanghai. There was no cloud in the sky, and it was a brilliant blue. For a moment, he had a traumatic flashback of standing at this spot six months ago, September 11, on a morning that looked eerily similar.

Yet, life goes on; the first daffodils were blooming, and the trees were in various stages of budding. Phoenix took a huge breath and coughed from the frigid air, a response that let him know he was still alive.

From his balcony, the city assaulted his senses. The manicured southern edge of Central Park spread below him, its pathways crisscrossing the late-winter landscape where patches of stubborn snow still clung to the shadows. The air carried that distinct Manhattan scent—the mineral coldness of late winter mixing with hot pretzels and roasting nuts from the vendors at the park's entrance.

The crystal-clear sky cast an early spring light across the cityscape—brilliant and sharp-edged, illuminating the copper rooftops of the pre-war buildings along Central Park South and causing the glass facades of Midtown skyscrapers to glitter like cut diamonds. It offered no warmth, only unforgiving lucidity that matched his mood.

Phoenix's body was still calibrated to Shanghai's gentle warmth. The biting cold made his fingers stiff as he walked back in and reluctantly called home, knowing it was morning there, even though his body was saying otherwise.

oooo

"Hello?" his wife's voice was clipped and distracted.

"Hey, it's me. I arrived from Shanghai a few minutes ago." Phoenix loosened his tie, sinking onto the edge of the bed.

"Oh, right. How was the flight?"

"Long. Listen, Pru, the deal went through. Better than we expected. The valuation—"

"That's nice," The sound of papers shuffling came through the line. "Did you remember to sign those documents for the church fundraising drive for the gymnasium expansion—before you left?"

Phoenix closed his eyes. "I've been gone two weeks."

"And I've been holding things together here. Reverend Edwards needs those signatures by tomorrow."

"The company could sell for much more than we dreamed, Pru. This could change everything."

There was a brief silence. "Change what, exactly?"

"Our future. We could do anything. Go anywhere."

"I have my women's ministry conference next month, where I'll speak to two hundred Christian women about family values."

Her voice hardened. "Not everyone wants their life upended, Phoenix."

"Right." He watched a plane's vapor trail dissipate across the sky. "How are the girls?"

"They are fine. Faith is organizing the teen mission work for the church youth group. Judith's dating the new associate minister."

Of course, they were. "Good for them."

"I need to go. The church leaders who make up our governing council are coming over to plan the outreach fundraiser."

Phoenix swallowed the words rising in his throat. "Don't let me keep you."

"Don't forget we have the Edwards over after church on Sunday." A pause. "Safe travels."

The line went dead before he could respond.

oooo

Phoenix stared at the phone for several minutes after hanging up with Prudence. The city pulsated beyond his window, alive in a way his marriage hadn't been for years. Twenty-five years of measured distance, of conversations that never penetrated the surface. She had married religion long before she'd married him, finding in its rigid certainties the security her childhood had never provided.

The daughter of a prominent pastor who'd criticized her relentlessly behind closed doors while presenting a perfect family image to his congregation, Prudence had learned early that safety lay in rules, in appearances, in never questioning what had been established as truth.

He couldn't remember the last time they'd shared more than perfunctory physical contact—a quick kiss on the cheek, a stiff hug in front of church friends.

His thoughts turned to his daughters. Faith, like her mother in her certainty, organized church youth programs with the same precision Prudence applied to fundraisers.

Yet he remembered the little girl who once asked why the stars couldn't be touched if God made them for people. That curiosity—where had it gone?

Dating the associate minister, Judith followed the approved path just as he had. He'd taught them success meant conformity, not by his words but by his example. The realization struck him: his greatest regret wasn't that they'd chosen their mother's path but that he'd never shown them there could be other paths worth taking.

oooo

He picked up the phone again, hesitated, then dialed. She answered on the second ring.

"I was hoping you'd call," her sultry voice starkly contrasted with the previous conversation.

"Lil," saying her name released tension in his chest, "I'm back."

"In your hotel?" There was interest in her voice.

"Yes. I spoke with Prudence."

A soft exhale. "How was that?"

"The usual." Phoenix moved to the minibar, phone cradled against his shoulder. "She's busy planning another fundraiser. Didn't ask about Shanghai."

"I want to know everything. Tell me about the deal."

Phoenix poured himself a scotch, settling into an armchair. His face relaxed. "It went better than expected. The Chinese investors were impressed with the projections. We're looking at an eight-figure valuation."

"Phoenix, that's incredible," Her voice dropped lower. "I'm so proud of you."

He closed his eyes, letting her words wash over him. "It's strange. I should be ecstatic, but all I could think about on the flight was ... what's it all for?"

"Ah, the existential crisis of the successful man," Lil said, but her tone was gentle and thoughtful. "Have you been reading that Camus I gave you?"

"Yes, nights and on the plane. You were right about it." He took a sip of scotch. "There's a line that keeps coming back to me about how we get in the habit of living before acquiring the habit of thinking."

"That's exactly what's happening to you." Soft music wafted in the background; she was probably surrounded by books and canvases in her studio. "You're finally thinking about your life."

"It's terrifying," he admitted.

"It's beautiful," she countered. "What did you feel, sitting across from those investors, knowing you'd built a business they valued highly?"

No one had asked him that. Not his partners, not his wife. "Empty," he said finally. "Accomplished, but hollow."

"That's because you're ready for a better reality." Her voice lowered. I miss your body. How you looked at me last time, like you saw aspects no one else could see."

Heat spread through him. "That's how it feels with you. Like I'm truly seen."

"You are," she said. "Everything about you—your doubts, your desires, even your darkness. Especially that."

Phoenix found himself smiling. "I never knew it could be like this. Not only the sex, though God, Lilith..." He trailed off.

"I know." He could hear the passion in her voice. "For me, too. It's everything else as well. The conversations afterward. The questions we ask together."

"Pru's never asked a difficult question in her life."

"That's why she's happy," Lil said without malice. "Certainty is comfortable. Questioning is messier."

"I keep thinking about leaving," he revealed, the words emerging before he could stop them.

A pause. "The company? Or Prudence?" Lilith asked.

"Both, maybe. Everything."

She was quiet for a moment. "You could, you know. With this deal, you could do anything."

Last autumn, she'd abruptly stopped mid-conversation in her studio, fixing him with that penetrating gaze that always made him feel transparent.

"You talk about leaving as if it's an event, Phoenix, not a process. You've been leaving for years—physically present in boardrooms and church pews while your mind wanders elsewhere."

Her words had stung with their accuracy. When he protested, she shook her head. "I'm not your escape route. When you walk through my door, I want all of you here because you've chosen to be, not because you're fleeing something else."

It was the first time he'd recognized that her fierce independence wasn't just attractive—it was essential to her survival in a world that constantly asked women to diminish themselves.

The possibilities hung between them, tantalizingly real. "If you could paint anything in the world right now, what would you paint?" he asked, changing direction.

"You," she said without hesitation. "Not how others see you, but how I see you. A man at the threshold, half in shadow, half in light. Beautiful because he's finally asking the questions he's always been afraid to ask."

Phoenix felt his heart beat faster. "I have to see you when I get back."

"Yes," she agreed. "My studio. Tuesday. Prudence has her Bible study."

"Tuesday," he repeated, already counting the hours.

"Phoenix?" Her voice softened further. "Whatever you decide about the company, about everything ... know I'm not afraid of your questions. Or mine."

After they hung up, Phoenix rose and stood at the window for a long time, watching the city buildings blur through what he was surprised to realize were tears.

oooo

The scotch had burned pleasantly but left him restless. Stepping onto the terrace, the March air carried enough cold to cut through his lingering jet lag. Manhattan spread before him—Central Park, a colorful rectangle against the glittering geometry of the city. He leaned against the brick banister, loosening his tie and letting it hang like a surrender flag.

Two phone calls. Two women. Two entirely different lives. Prudence hadn't asked a single question about Shanghai. Lilith wanted to know everything about the business deal and his feelings while making it. Prudence scheduled church events during his absences; Lilith sent him Camus to read on the plane. The contrast left him dizzy, or was it the eighteen-hour flight and twenty-year-old scotch?

He'd met Lilith at a fundraiser three years ago, where she'd been invited to paint live during the program. While everyone else had praised her "gift from God," she'd confessed to him later, over coffee, that she found the whole experience stifling. "They want art that answers questions," she'd said. "I'm interested in art, which asks them." That conversation had revealed another soul similarly trapped between worlds.

Their affair had begun as an intellectual one. Books were exchanged discreetly. There followed discussions about existentialism, Sartre, and de Beauvoir, as well as finding meaning in a world without a predetermined purpose.

When it grew physical six months later, the seamlessness of the transition stunned him. In her studio, between torrid bouts of lovemaking that left him more satisfied than he'd ever been, they would lie sweaty and naked, discussing philosophy, art, and the nature of reality—all the questions he'd once found so alive before his church and business had taught him to fear them.

He thought of Lilith in her studio—paint-spattered hands gesturing emphatically as she argued Camus' points, her dark curls pulled back haphazardly with a pencil thrust through them, those reading glasses she refused to wear in public perched precariously on her nose.

Unlike Prudence's carefully curated appearance, Lilith wore her body like a comfortable home rather than a display case. The casual way she smudged paint across her forehead without noticing, her laughter when he pointed it out—"My canvas extends beyond the frame, Phoenix," —these were the details he found himself missing most during his travels.

"What are we doing?" he once asked, guilt momentarily overwhelming the pleasure.

"Living," she'd answered. "We are living."

But they both had children. Both had spouses. Both were embedded in a religious community where divorce was taboo. Their stolen afternoons remained precious but ultimately insufficient—islands of authenticity in lives otherwise defined by compromise.

Now, the deal was done. Freedom printed on bank statements. The culmination of twenty years of relentless work—building a company from nothing, proving everyone from his small-town doubters to his disapproving father-in-law wrong.

And yet.

Pushing away from the balustrade, he began pacing the length of the terrace. Five steps one way, turn, five steps back—the ritual of the caged.

The irony wasn't lost on him. He'd spent twenty years building a company that promised freedom through success, yet here he was, trapped in the same metrics-driven existence he sold to clients. Eight figures. That's what his life had been reduced to—an evaluation not of his humanity but of his market value.

The business world had taught him to commodify himself and to view his worth through the endless cycle of proving his value through numbers. Manhattan spread before him—a monument to commerce, every gleaming surface reflecting ambition and acquisition.

He'd navigated its competitive currents expertly, yet what had he sacrificed to stay afloat? His true interests, his creativity, the parts of himself that couldn't be monetized or leveraged for shareholder value. Corporate culture demanded a specific performance—projecting confidence, making swift decisions, climbing relentlessly upward—while brutally punishing any display of vulnerability, uncertainty, or resistance to the system.

What would Prudence say if he left? The business and —her. Would she even be surprised? They'd been performing their marriage for years, and sometimes, he wondered if she, too, was waiting for the curtain to fall. The thought should have been liberating. Instead, it hollowed him out.

And his daughters. Jude dating a pastor, and Faith leading church service projects. They'd chosen their mother's certainty over his questions. Would they choose her in a divorce, too? The thought of losing them tore him apart.

He pulled his phone from his pocket, checking the time—5 p.m.

I should call Marcus. If anyone would understand this flavor of success-induced emptiness, it would be him. Their friendship—if you could call it that—had been forged in luxury hotel bars across four continents.

It was a relationship built on confidences exchanged in the safe spaces between business and personal life. Marcus had sold his tech company three years ago. He'd gotten out, somehow, with no regrets.

Phoenix dialed before he could reconsider.

oooo

"The prodigal businessman returns to New York," Marcus answered, ambient noise suggesting he was out somewhere, "how was Shanghai?"

"Successful." Phoenix sank into the terrace chaise lounge, eyes fixed on the skyline. "The deal's going through."

"Congratulations. You should be celebrating."

"True. I should be."

A knowing pause. "Hmm. That feeling."

"What feeling?"

"When you finally catch what you've been chasing, only to discover it's not what you wanted after all." Marcus's voice softened. "I've been there."

Exhaling slowly, Phoenix said, "I'm thinking of getting out. Selling the company."

"Okay, and then what?"

The question hung in the air, unanswerable. "I don't know."

"That's the hardest part," Marcus said. "The what comes next. Listen, you need a place to think that isn't that sterile hotel room or some overpriced Midtown bar."

"I'm not in the mood for crowds."

"Not crowds. Something else entirely." The sound of Marcus stepping away from the background noise. "There's a place. No sign, only a door. 111 Janus Street. Knock twice, pause, then once more. Use the secret passphrase "Janus faces forward."

"A bar?" Phoenix asked skeptically.

"Not exactly. Let's call it ... a space between spaces. For people asking the questions you're asking."

Marcus's tone caught Phoenix's attention. "What kind of questions?"

"The kind that can't be answered with balance sheets or sermon points." A laugh in Marcus's voice. "Try the absinthe."

oooo

After hanging up, Phoenix stood at the edge of the terrace, looking down at the ant-like figures moving along Fifth Avenue. Each contained a universe of doubts and desires, successes and failures. The physical and emotional wounds of 9/11, the previous September, were still evident.

Like the Twin Towers, he had meticulously built his life, floor by floor: the right schools, the right wife, the right business, the proper church position—a perfect construction. Now, at age forty-seven, he could see the cracks in the foundation spreading, threatening collapse.

Returning to his room, he changed from his business suit into dark jeans and a cashmere sweater. He studied his reflection—the gray at his temples, the lines around his eyes that hadn't been there five years ago.

"111 Janus Street," he whispered as if issuing a challenge. He slipped his wallet into his pocket, left the safety of The Plaza, and stepped into the Manhattan night; not entirely sure what he was looking for but convinced he couldn't find it where he'd already been.

# CHAPTER TWO

## The Unmarked Door

The leather seat of the Town Car seemed to envelop Phoenix as he sank into it, the cabin's warmth a stark contrast to the brisk March air. The driver, a Sikh man with a dark blue turban, neatly combed beard, and eyes that had seen everything the city could offer, pulled away from The Plaza's illuminated awning.

"One-eleven Janus Street, please. Do you know it?" Phoenix asked.

Their eyes met in the rearview mirror.

"I think I do, sir. That's down in the old Meatpacking District. Not many people are going there at this hour." The driver paused, registering Phoenix's attire—too expensive for the usual destinations in that area. "Special occasion?"

"I'm meeting a friend." The lie came easily after decades of practice. Friend, wife, lover—the roles were beginning to jumble.

oooo

Prudence would be at home now, sitting in her pristine office, organizing the next church capital campaign, a cup of tea gone cold at her elbow. Lilith's earlier text flashed in his mind: Just thinking of you. The studio misses you, too.

Peering out the window, the car glided south past Hell's Kitchen on Ninth Avenue. His body was in New York, but his mind remained suspended somewhere over the Pacific, between Shanghai's success and whatever awaited him on Janus Street. Three phone calls in the span of an hour—each pulling him in different directions like stars trying to claim a wayward planet.

Prudence's crisp dismissal. Lilith's thoughtful intimacy. Marcus' cryptic invitation.

The city had changed since his visit six months ago. American flags hung from apartment balconies, office windows, and construction scaffolding—some new and vibrant, others faded from months of sun and rain but still proudly displayed. "NEVER FORGET" signs appeared sporadically, silent testaments to wounds still fresh.

A city transformed by absence. Phoenix knew about that kind of transformation.

The car turned west, cutting across the grid of Manhattan, streetlights shrouded by the fog that had begun rolling in from the Hudson. He checked his watch—7:12 p.m. Jet lag was hitting him in waves now, fatigue followed by strange moments of clear thought.

oooo

"You visiting from out of town?" the driver asked, breaking the silence.

"Yes, I flew in after closing a deal in Shanghai. My body is still in their time zone."

The driver sighed sagely. "Business. The world keeps spinning. After September, many people think everything stops. Oh no. We adapt."

Studying the man's profile, Phoenix asked, "Do things ever change, though? Or do we convince ourselves they have?"

The question emerged spontaneously, too revealing for a conversation with a stranger. Yet the anonymity of the backseat, the time between destinations, unlocked inhibitions.

The driver regarded this, unperturbed by the philosophical turn. "Both, maybe. The river is never the same water, but always the same river."

oooo

As they pressed deeper into Lower Manhattan, the architecture morphed around them. The gleaming towers of

Midtown gave way to older structures—cast-iron facades, repurposed warehouses, and cobblestone streets that remembered horse-drawn carriages. The fog thickened, softening the edges of buildings and transforming streetlights into diffuse halos.

Here, the city appeared older and mysterious. Phoenix thought of Lil's words—"a man at the threshold, half in shadow, half in light." The Meatpacking District at night embodied that liminality—its industrial past still visible around the first tentative signs of transformation.

Lilith's paintings hung on no church walls. Her canvases explored in-between spaces, blurring boundaries between elements. "I'm interested in enantiodromia—the tendency of things to transform into their opposites," she'd told him once, stepping back from a canvas where blues and reds met without clear demarcation. "The moment before decision, the space between certainty and doubt. That's where all possibility lives."

The critics called her work "disquieting" and "challenging," terms she wore as badges of honor. "If art doesn't disquiet," she'd say, eyes flashing, "what's the point?"

oooo

The car slowed as they entered a gritty street of brick structures. Once-bustling loading docks now stood empty, their rolling doors closed forever. A few high-end restaurants and fashion shops had established footholds in the area, their glowing interiors visible through fogged windows, but most buildings remained dark.

"Getting close now, I think," the driver said, navigating the increasingly narrow streets. "Strange place for meeting friends."

Phoenix didn't respond. His attention had fixed on a nondescript brick building at the end of the block. There was no sign, and no address was visible from the street. A wooden door was recessed into the decaying wall, illuminated by a irregular light above it. Was it the jet lag, or did the door quiver in the fog as if alive?

The car rolled to a stop."One-eleven Janus Street," the driver announced, a note of uncertainty as he peered through the windshield. "At least, should be. Strange, no number."

Handing over the credit card, Phoenix added a generous cash tip when the transaction was complete. "Thank you. I can make my way from here."

"Want me to wait? Not many cabs in this area."

"No need." Phoenix stepped out into the fog, which immediately beaded on his cashmere sweater. "I'm not sure how long I'll be."

The driver's concern flashed briefly across his features. "Be careful, sir. Funny things happen in this district."

The Town Car pulled away, its taillights quickly swallowed by the fog. Phoenix stood alone on the cobblestone street, the silence broken only by the distant hum of the city and the muted dripping of water from fire escapes above.

oooo

Phoenix Adams moved with the command of a man accustomed to authority, his six-foot frame maintaining a rigidity that had become second nature after decades of performance. At forty-seven, his dark hair had surrendered to distinguished silver at the temples, creating a contrast that spoke of experience rather than age. His face bore the markers of constant evaluation—fine lines radiating from eyes that had squinted at too many spreadsheets, a furrow between his brows that deepened when he wasn't consciously relaxing it.

His hands, with neatly manicured nails, often betrayed what his face concealed. Fingers tightened around pen caps as stress sought release or curled into loose fists when at rest, never fully relaxed. Phoenix dressed with calculated thought, his wardrobe an armor of understated wealth. Even in casual clothes, as he was tonight, his presentation remained deliberate.

His body beneath these carefully selected garments told its tale—a physique maintained through disciplined sessions at hotel gyms across four continents, with muscles toned but not overdone.

When he moved through the world, Phoenix did so with purpose rather than pleasure, each stride economical, his gaze focused on destinations rather than journeys. Yet beneath this carefully constructed exterior lived traces of the boy who had once written stories under blanket forts, who had spent hours watching clouds transform above Appalachian ridges.

oooo

That boy still lived in the laugh lines that appeared genuine and unexpected on the rare occasions when Phoenix forgot to monitor his responses—a true self buried beneath layers of expectation and performance that seemed to stir as he approached the unmarked door on Janus Street, each footstep echoing between the brick walls of the narrow street.

No sign indicated what lay beyond. No nameplate was posted for prospective patrons. Only the door itself—richly grained walnut with a small brass mail slot positioned at eye level and a simple brass knocker that gleamed dully in the fog-diffused illumination.

Raising his hand, Phoenix remembered Marcus's instructions. Two knocks. Pause. One more.

His knuckles had barely brushed the wood when doubt flooded him. What was he doing here? What did he expect to find behind this door that he hadn't seen—in Shanghai's success, Prudence's ordered world, or even Lil's passionate embrace?

Still, he knocked. Firmly. Twice in succession, a deliberate pause, then once more.

"The sound disappeared into the fog. For a moment, nothing happened—finally, the brass mail slot opened with a soft metallic creak. Phoenix could see nothing through the rectangular opening—only darkness and the sense of being observed.

"Yes?" a voice, neither male nor female, neither young nor old, emerged from the darkness.

Phoenix hesitated. In his exhaustion, he struggled to remember the passphrase. He cleared his throat. "Marcus Ryan sent me."

A pause. "What did Mr. Ryan tell you to say once here?"

The voice was patient, expectant.

Marcus had said something about Janus, about spaces between spaces. His mind racing, he said, "Janus faces forward," the words emerging from some intuitive place he hadn't known existed.

The mail slot closed. For a terrible moment, Phoenix thought he'd failed some existential test. Almost imperceptibly, the walnut door receded inward inch by inch. No creak, no sound at all—an invitation into darkness.

oooo

As the unmarked door opened fully, he entered a world that seemed to exist outside of time. The speakeasy unfolded before him in layers of amber beam and shadow, an intimate oasis insulated from the city's relentless pace.

Crystal chandeliers hung from the coffered ceiling; their blaze deliberately dimmed to create pools of soothing illumination. Copious candles made it warm and flickering. The walls were paneled in burled walnut and richly grained; they seemed to move in the low gleam, occasionally interrupted by alcoves housing small sculptures or single paintings that could have been the center-piece of any museum collection.

The air carried complex aromas: the sweetness of aged cognac, the earthiness of tobacco, the tang of polished brass, and a faint herbal scent that Phoenix couldn't iden-tify but that seemed to sharpen his senses. The room breathed wealth, but not the ostentatious kind that shout-ed its arrogance. This ambiance evidenced old money, pa-tient money, that had survived empires and revolutions.

A curved bar dominated one side of the room, its ma-hogany surface burnished to a mirror finish by decades of use and careful polishing. Behind it, antiqued mirrors and vintage bottles gleamed like jewels—not the expected top-shelf brands, but hand-labeled vessels in shapes Phoenix had never seen, some appearing centuries old. With slate streaks in her dark hair, the mixologist worked with monastic concentration and artistic movements.

Around the room, leather booths created private is-lands of conversation, each separated from its neighbors by clever architectural details that prevented sound from traveling. The patrons were few—a dozen or so—and they spoke in hushed tones, their faces animated but their voices controlled. They appeared to be cosmopolitan aes-thetes sipping absinthe and probably arguing about art.

There were no trendy smartphone conversations, only the gentle percussion of ice in shakers, the soft clink of glassware, and the muffled sounds of the city beyond the thick walls. It could have been a bar in 1920s Paris.

A discreet sign from the doorkeeper guided him to a secluded alcove where a leather wingback chair waited. Its arms were burnished to a honeyed patina by countless elbows. As he sank into it, the leather seemed to embrace him with a yielding firmness that his body immediately recognized as home.

His spine, rigid with the accumulated stress of transpacific flights and weeks of negotiations, softened vertebra by vertebra. For the first time since landing in New York—for the first time in years—his shoulders descended from their permanent position near his ears, the muscles releasing, causing an audible sigh. The tension that had become a familiar companion uncoiled from the base of his spine, causing his fingers to uncurl from their habitual half-fists.

oooo

"Good evening," the voice came from someone who had appeared beside him without sound or warning. Phoenix startled, his hand instinctively grabbing the arm of the chair as his head jerked toward the source. The momentary surprise melted instantly as he found himself regarded by eyes that seemed to contain an internal glow.

The server's features were a perfect study in beautiful contradictions—a strong jaw but full lips, broad shoulders tapering to narrow hips, delicate wrists emerging from rolled sleeves. Phoenix couldn't have assigned a definitive gender to the person if asked, only an unmistakable beauty that transcended such categories.

"I'm Dion. Welcome to our oasis," his name was proffered with a slight bow that was theatrical yet utterly sincere. "Might I suggest a libation, or do you have a prefer-ence?"

Phoenix found his voice, his dry throat working visi-bly before the words came. "My name is Phoenix. Phoenix Adams." The words emerged huskier than in-tended. A flush crept up his neck—an emotion between embarrassment and a more complex sensation. "I'd wel-come a suggestion. It's been quite a day." He shook his head and sighed as if trying to encompass the enormity of what that simple phrase contained.

Dion's mouth revealed a slight asymmetry that ele-vated the beauty of his face instead of diminishing it. Phoenix found his attention drawn momentarily to the server's lips—perfectly formed, neither too full nor too thin, and possessed of an expressive quality that seemed to communicate as much as the words themselves.

"I believe I have what you need—it awaits your dis-covery. Allow me to prepare the elixir, and I'll return mo-mentarily."

As Dion moved away, Phoenix surrendered himself to the room, his body settling deeper into the chair with the exhale of someone consciously relinquishing control. From his alcove, he could observe without being ob-served—a prospect that appealed deeply to the person who had spent decades on display. The perpetual perfor-mance of competence that tightened the muscles around his eyes relaxed, allowing his gaze to soften and wander.

Voices murmured from other alcoves, creating an acoustic texture that provided privacy without isolation. The lights adjusted like magic, dimming to create a more intimate sphere. Phoenix ran his fingers along the edge of the small marble-topped table beside him, his touch lingering and exploratory like a blind person reading Braille. He noted how the veining in the stone had been positioned to mirror the grain of the wooden floor beneath—a refined detail that could only have been born of obsessive care.

Responsiveness spread through him that had nothing to do with the ambient temperature. It began in his solar plexus and radiated outward, causing his chest to expand as if making room for long-absent pleasures. His breathing deepened, shifting from the shallow, rapid pattern of perpetual vigilance to a more relaxed pace. It was the excitement of recognition—of finding oneself in a place created by and for people who worship at the altar of beauty.

Phoenix had visited the most exclusive restaurants in Asia and the most expensive hotels in Europe, but this place was different. It didn't flaunt its elegance but wore it with a casual confidence that had never considered being otherwise. His jaw habitually clenched to maintain his public face, softened enough that his lips parted.

Dion reappeared, carrying a silver tray holding a single glass of transcendent green spirit. The glass was a work of art—handblown crystal with a delicate flare at the rim. A small silver-slotted spoon lay across its top. Beside it sat a sugar cube and a small crystal carafe of water on a linen cloth.

"Absinthe," Dion announced reverently, setting the tray on the marble surface with balletic precision, "not the counterfeit versions that flooded the market after the ban, but the genuine article—distilled from recipes preserved by families who refused to let beauty die by legislative decree."

As Phoenix watched, Dion placed the sugar cube on the slotted spoon, dripping water over it with ritualistic patience. The liquid below clouded gradually, releasing a bouquet of anise and elusive botanicals.

"Our proprietor, Mircea, believes that certain experiences should be preserved," Dion continued, low enough that Phoenix craned closer to catch the words. "This establishment exists to offer sanctuary to those experiences—and to the people capable of appreciating them."

He handed the transformed drink to Phoenix. "Our owner collects objects of beauty, but more importantly, he curates moments. By an unusual coincidence, he's here this evening and mentioned he might pay his respects if you're amenable."

Holding the glass, Phoenix noticed how the drink seemed to glow from within. "Mircea? That name is familiar somehow."

"Connections have a way of revealing themselves here," Dion said with an engaging look. "Do you know the word synchronicity, Mr. Adams? Synchronicity implies a meaningful coincidence—when two or more events that aren't causally connected occur together in a way that feels significant rather than random chance. This place exists at the intersection of intention and synchronicity."

"That is fascinating. And Dion, please call me Phoenix."

oooo

As Dion departed with another slight bow, Phoenix raised the glass to his lips, his hand steady but his pulse quickening with anticipation. The first sip spread across his palate like a revelation—complex, botanical, with a touch of bitterness but an underlying sweetness that emerged gradually. His eyelids fluttered and closed involuntarily, his facial muscles softening in an expression of unexpected pleasure. The alcohol traveled down his throat and bloomed outward from his center, a warmth that seemed to illuminate him from within, causing his skin to prickle.

He settled into the chair. Knots of strain in his lower back seem to dissolve, causing a half sigh, half moan to escape his mouth. His fingers relaxed their grip on the glass, holding it now with barely enough pressure to keep it secure. Phoenix felt right where he should be for the first time in a long time, though he couldn't have explained why. His breath slowed, matching the pace of the room. His forehead relaxed, and his countenance softened. The foreign sensations took him a few moments to recognize: peace.

# CHAPTER THREE

## Mircea's Recognition

Taking his third sip of absinthe, Phoenix sensed a presence approaching. There was a change in the room's atmosphere, as if the air was making way for someone. He looked up to find a tall figure standing at the edge of his alcove, white hair gleaming in the subdued light. The man's tailored suit hung with such a perfect drape that it might have been liquid midnight poured over his frame. His hands, emerging from French cuffs secured with amber cufflinks, carried the elegant ease of grace that comes only from decades of assured existence.

"May I join you?" he asked in a cultivated baritone voice, its accent hard to place. European indeed, but with a malleability that suggested fluency in myriad languages.

Phoenix instinctively stood. "I'd be honored."

"Mircea Vasilescu."

Extending his hand, "Phoenix Adams."

After a firm handshake, Mircea settled into the chair with collected grace. His eyes—pure silver that seemed to hold light differently than ordinary eyes—studied Phoenix with quiet intensity. The slight furrowing at their corners suggested not an introduction but recognition struggling to surface.

His distinctive scent was not a commercial cologne but more refined. Aged sandalwood mingled with rare oud and hints of Moroccan saffron, creating smells of distant markets and exclusive European ateliers. It was the kind of fragrance that couldn't be bought off a shelf—it spoke of a man who moved effortlessly between Byzantine monasteries and Parisian perfumeries, valuing the unique over the expensive.

There was an odd feeling of familiarity. It recalled what Phoenix had witnessed years before in a garden half a world away. His pulse quickened, pleasant memories flooding his mind.

"We've met," they said simultaneously.

A smile spread across Mircea's face—not the practiced social expression Phoenix had grown accustomed to in business circles, but a genuineness that accentuated his austere features. "Asolo," Mircea said. "The Cipriani. You were admiring Titian's light at sunset."

Memory cascaded through Phoenix—a perfect Italian evening, the scent of jasmine mingling with tobacco, the patio chair still holding the day's heat. "The garden," he said, nostalgic. "Black truffle season."

"White," Mircea corrected gently. "The rarest. The chef had prepared a risotto that evening that I still dream of." He made a small circle with his fingers as if recapturing a morsel of that remembered dish. "You were there for a brief holiday if I recall. Yet your mind seemed elsewhere."

Phoenix's eyes widened involuntarily. The details of that evening had acquired a dreamlike quality over the years, but now they crystallized into perfect memory. "You were smoking a cigar. One I'd never encountered before."

"A Davidoff Dom Pérignon," Mircea affirmed. "Discontinued in the early nineties. I still have a few remaining from the original release in my humidor."

"You invited me to join you." Phoenix's fingers twitched at the memory, muscles recalling the unfamiliar weight of that rare cigar.

"We talked about .... "

"Beauty," Mircea finished for him. "You understood what most never grasp—the soul that appreciates beauty may sometimes walk alone."

Observing a tingling rising from his chest to his face, Phoenix experienced the physical manifestation of being understood. The conversation had affected him profoundly, and he'd mentioned it to no one—not Prudence, who would have dismissed it as pretentious nonsense; not colleagues, who would have reduced it to networking; not even Lilith, with whom he shared his deepest thoughts. It had remained private, a secret feast he occasionally revisited in moments of doubt.

"You were there to acquire a fresco," Phoenix recalled, the detail surfacing through years of buried memory.

Mircea's eyebrows rose marginally, the only indication of his surprise at Phoenix's recall. "From a small cathedral in Treviso. An altarpiece attributed to a student of Lotto. The church needed funds for restoration, and I needed ..." He paused, searching for the definitive word. "Beauty."

The word hung between them, its multiple meanings creating harmonics. "And now here you are, in one of my sanctuaries." Mircea turned elegantly to encompass the speakeasy. "Connections have a way of revealing themselves in this place. We might now recognize what you called coincidence in Asolo as synchronicity."

"Dion mentioned a similar observation," Phoenix looked at the absinthe in his hand, its green transparency now clouded to opalescence.

"Yes, Dion perceives much," Mircea said, a note of affection warming his sentiment. "Indeed, this space exists at the intersection of intention and synchronicity. Those who find their way here are rarely guided by chance alone."

He studied Phoenix with those fervent eyes that seemed to penetrate layers beneath the visible. "You're at a threshold, I think. As you were in that garden, though you might not have recognized it then." Mircea's perception was unnervingly accurate.

"The business deal in Shanghai," Phoenix began, falling back into the familiar territory of his professional identity. His mouth tightened, making his next breath audible in the quiet alcove.

Mircea waved dismissively, his hand cutting through the air with gentle finality. "The deal merely confirmed feelings that have been forming for years." His gaze didn't waver. "Tell me, Phoenix, what do you hunger for that success cannot feed?"

The question bypassed Phoenix's usual defenses, striking directly at the core of the emptiness he'd been carrying. His eyes focused on Mircea's face, showing a vulnerability that hadn't been visible since he'd entered the speakeasy. "I don't know," he whispered, the words emerging as barely more than an exhale.

Then, more firmly, with an honesty that Mircea's direct gaze seemed to demand. "No, that's not true. I do know. But I don't have words for it yet."

Mircea's satisfaction was evident by the pleasure on his face. "It's time you discovered those words."

He moved nearer, his mood intensifying without any perceptible change in his expression. "I have a private room here—a collection of sorts. Things I've gathered over a lifetime of searching for the same nameless hunger you're feeling. Would you be interested in experiencing it?"

A slight tremor passed through Phoenix's hands, causing ripples in his absinthe. It was not fear but anticipation—the physical response to standing at the edge of a momentous opportunity. "I'd be honored," Phoenix said, surprising himself with the formality of his response as if some deeper part of him recognized the ritual nature of what his host was offering.

Mircea's approval reached his singular eyes. "Excellent. Finish your drink. Please take your time. Dion will guide you when you're ready." He rose, then paused, looking down at Phoenix. "There's only one condition to entering my private sanctum."

Phoenix looked up questioningly.

"Everything within is complimentary—the rarest books, the finest spirits, art pieces thought lost to history—all available for your enjoyment, with one stipulation: you must do everything Dion asks of you." Mircea's expression remained enigmatic and complex to read. "Do you accept these terms?"

Without fully understanding why, Phoenix's head moved in assent, his body deciding before his mind could analyze it. "I accept."

"I shall see you there shortly." Mircea touched Phoenix lightly on the arm as he departed—an intimate and consecrating pressure.

As Mircea's figure receded into the speakeasy's ambient twilight, Phoenix exhaled, unaware that he had been holding his breath. He carefully lifted the absinthe to his lips and finished the last drops, the complex botanicals tasting like possibility itself.

# Interlude - Mircea's Essence

The name "Mircea Vasilescu" recurs in rumors across time, though never in official records. Those who've encountered him describe a man whose eyes reflect timelessness as if he sees the world through a different lens than ordinary people.

Mircea was born in the Carpathian Mountains of Romania, though the exact date remains a mystery. His childhood unfolded in a remote village where the boundary between the physical and spiritual worlds remained permeable, elders still practiced rituals predating Christianity, and he learned that reality was far more expansive than most perceived.

He witnessed his village's destruction during one of the countless waves of religious persecution that swept across Eastern Europe, forcing the youth to flee his homeland carrying only a wooden chest containing manuscripts in languages few could read. His unique silver eyes—inherited from his mother, who was said to converse with forest spirits and understand the language of dreams—marked him as unique from birth.

In Florence during the Renaissance, Mircea surfaced as a young collector with an uncanny eye for beauty and meaning. Artists and philosophers were drawn to him for his insights. He moved among the Medici court with quiet confidence, often seen in conversation with Botticelli or seated at a café with Leonardo da Vinci, discussing how dreams and reality frequently mirror each other.

"Beauty isn't decoration," he would say, "but a key that unlocks doors within ourselves."

In the early 1900s, Mircea established himself in Vienna, where a young Carl Jung encountered him while exploring the unconscious mind. Jung later described meeting "a silver-eyed Romanian whose understanding of symbols and alchemy predated my theories by what seemed centuries." Jung reportedly refined aspects of his concepts of the collective unconscious, archetypes, and dreams after lengthy conversations with Mircea in a Viennese café.

The 1920s found him in Paris among the Lost Generation. Hemingway described Mircea in private letters: "He listened with his whole body. No man ever heard me better." Fitzgerald once wrote, "I remember thinking, as Mr. Vasilescu gazed across Gertrude Stein's cluttered apartment, that he seemed neither lost nor searching.

While we chased the new, Mircea carried something immeasurably ancient within him."

Stein invited him regularly to her salon, where his conversations with James Joyce about dreams and symbols reportedly influenced passages in *Finnegans Wake*.

Picasso's portrait of Mircea was created in a single sitting in the artist's Montmartre studio. When pressed about the strange duality of the image—Mircea's face simultaneously reveals serene presence and ancient knowledge—Picasso would only shrug.

"I painted the man who exists outside time," he told a persistent collector who offered a fortune for the canvas. "Some works are not meant for gallery walls." The portrait remains the only Picasso never photographed for catalogs or displayed in exhibitions. It now hangs above the bar in the private room of the Speakeasy.

The Purging Room has existed in various forms throughout Mircea's journey—sometimes in a Viennese apartment, sometimes a Parisian atelier, and now in a restored warehouse in New York.

It was in Paris that Mircea encountered Dion, then a young street performer whose natural grace and instinctual understanding of beauty caught his attention. Their relationship defied simple definitions—mentor and protégé, sometimes lovers, and sometimes partners curating and guiding mystical experiences for others. Where Mircea embodies conscious intellect, Dion possesses intuitive discernment; together, they personify the Celtic ideal of *anam cara*, soul friends.

How Mircea has lived so long remains unexplained, yet his purpose remains consistent: creating spaces where people approaching personal thresholds can discover wholeness. His collection of beautiful art, literature, spirits, and mysterious artifacts serves not as possessions but as bridges—objects that help others transform their perception of the world and themselves.

Mircea recognized turbulence in Phoenix Adams in Asolo years before their encounter in Manhattan—a soul divided against itself, standing at the brink where transformation becomes possible. The "coincidental" reunion was foreshadowed in their lucid dreams and deepest longings.

The Purging Room exists in liminal spaces, accessible only to those who most need it. Within its circular walls, time moves differently, and the confines between the inner and outer worlds become thin enough for actual change to begin.

"There are doors," Mircea once told Hemingway during a late night at Les Deux Magots, "that appear only when you're ready to walk through them. And what waits on the other side is nothing more than your true self, the one you've always been beneath the masks."

# CHAPTER FOUR

## Crossing The Threshold

D ion reappeared at Phoenix's side with the silent grace of a dancer performing a ballet position. "If you'll follow me," he said, pitched above a whisper, "Mircea has prepared the room for your visit."

Rising, Phoenix's legs were unsteady beneath him—partly from the absinthe, partly from anticipation. He followed Dion through the speakeasy, past alcoves where other patrons engaged in fervent conversations, toward a corridor he hadn't noticed before. At its end stood a door of dark walnut banded with bronze, its surface carved with intricate patterns that fluctuated as they approached. Phoenix stood frozen, his muscle system momentarily forgetting its function.

"The Purging Room," Dion announced, producing a skeleton key of tarnished brass. As he unlocked the door, he turned to Phoenix, his expression serious. "Whatever happens within, whatever is asked of you, you must comply. This is Mircea's only condition for entry. You are offered what few have experienced. Do you give your word?"

Phoenix's pulse quickened, thudding audibly in his ears. "I give my word," he said, the formal phrase emerging from some more elemental, more genuine part of himself than the corporate platitudes he typically offered.

Dion bowed, then pulled the door open, standing close to Phoenix, creating an intimate space. The proximity felt good, but he couldn't pinpoint why.

Phoenix stepped across the threshold and immediately halted, his body losing momentum again as his senses struggled to process what lay before him. Where the speakeasy had been impressive, this was transcendent—a perfect circle of a room that seemed to exist outside of time. His eyes widened, pupils dilating to their fullest extent as they sought to absorb every detail.

The domed ceiling above portrayed a night sky unlike any he had seen on Earth—constellations from different hemispheres impossibly coexisting amid what appeared to be celestial bodies. Their soft glow illuminated the room in lights reminiscent of the fireflies of his childhood. The mystical configuration seemed like a bridge between the living and the spirit world.

The room's curved walls were lined with dark wood bookshelves that gleamed with the patina of reverent care.

At the four cardinal points, artworks were inset into the shelves, immersing Phoenix in feelings of awe. He vividly perceived his smallness amid the wonder of this expansive and magnificent room. The sensory details of the room were so immersive that they were almost dizzying.

"The Four Essentials of Being," Dion said quietly, "Mircea chose these masterworks especially for you."

To the North, da Vinci's *Battle of Anghiari*—the lost masterpiece that was thought to have vanished beneath later frescoes in Florence's Palazzo Vecchio. The culmination of Leonardo's study of human curiosity, motion, and intellectual passion captured in a moment of terrible beauty."

Dion's hand moved to indicate the Eastern point. "There, Raimondi's *Position Eight* from I Modi's *The Sixteen Pleasures*—presumed destroyed by Papal decree in 1524, yet preserved here in its original and sensual glory. An intimate moment where eyes meet during the physical union, desire and connection unified in a single gaze."

He continued clockwise. "To the South, the original *Scream* by Munch, thought to be lost forever. It was his first true vision of existential anguish before later versions diluted its raw emotional truth. The purest expression of affect, of feeling made visible, that humanity has produced."

Finally, Dion's hand completed the circle. "To the West, Klimt's original *Philosophy* mural—commissioned for Vienna University in 1900—was rejected for its radical vision of human consciousness and thought to have been destroyed by fire in 1945. In its swirling cosmic patterns and luminous human figures, Klimt captured the spirit of individual perception, waking consciousness, and finite existence with infinite potential."

His hand rose involuntarily to his chest, Phoenix pressing against his sternum as if to contain the expansion within it. His lips opened, but no words emerged.

Dion turned back to Phoenix. "Together, they represent the transformation Mircea offers—mind, body, soul, and spirit reunited after centuries of artificial separation."

At the room's center stood two leather armchairs facing each other, a few feet apart. They weren't identical—one in oxblood leather bore the impressions of countless sittings, while the midnight blue opposite remained firmer, less used. Beside each, a dark walnut table with an exquisite marble inlay top held an antique silver tray with a small water carafe and linen napkins.

The bar drew Phoenix's attention next—curved along one wall section, its surface inlaid with a translucent fossil resin that caught the glimmer from above. Behind it stood bottles that could not exist: pre-phylloxera Bordeaux, Chartreuse from before the monks were expelled from France, and absinthes from distilleries closed for over a century.

"Any spirit you've dreamed of sampling is yours to enjoy," Dion said, following Phoenix's stare. "Mircea believes experiences should be savored, not merely cataloged."

Phoenix was mute, his throat too constricted with emotion to form words. He moved toward the bookshelves, drawn by an irresistible gravitational pull. His fingers trembled as they hovered near the spines, afraid to touch what shouldn't still exist.

There was Hemingway's lost suitcase of manuscripts, recovered and bound. There were the complete plays of Sophocles, not only the seven that survived. There were the lost books of Euclid's *Elements*. There was the whole *Book of Thoth*. There were impeccably preserved First Editions signed by authors centuries dead. And, impossibly, books that were thought lost forever along with the Library of Alexandria.

"How?" Phoenix finally managed, the single syllable emerging hoarse and inadequate.

"Mircea has collected for many lifetimes," Dion replied, the deliberate ambiguity of the phrase hanging in the starlit atmosphere.

Moving around the room's circumference, Phoenix's fingers brushed lightly over selected spines, his breath catching each time he recognized a title he'd thought forever beyond reach. Four books seemed to respond physically to his touch: Beatrix Potter's privately published first printing of *The Tale of Peter Rabbit*, Pauline Réage's *Story of O* in its original French edition, Silvan Tomkins' handwritten manuscript of *Affect Imagery Consciousness*, and John O'Donohue's *Anam Cara*, which contained his reflections on Celtic spirituality and the philosophy of freedom.

Phoenix collected these four volumes without knowing why, cradling them against his chest like precious artifacts. Their weight was substantial and somehow alive against his ribcage.

"Your selections are fascinating," Dion observed, neutral but his eyes knowing. "Or would it be more accurate to say their selection of you?"

Phoenix's eyebrows lifted in question.

"Books have their own intentions," Dion said. He moved to the bar, preparing cocktails in delicate hand-blown coupe glasses with the ritualistic precision Phoenix had observed earlier. "Mircea invites you to stay as long as you wish. The night is yours. Please, be seated."

Settling into the oxblood chair, Phoenix felt it conform to his body as if it had been waiting specifically for him. The leather creaked softly beneath him—an intimate sound that raised goosebumps along his forearms. He carefully placed the four books on the side table, his fingers lingering on their covers.

"Dion," he said as the young man reached the bar, "thank you." He turned, and momentarily, Phoenix saw ancient discernment in his eyes that belied his youthful appearance—wisdom born of countless cycles of reconstruction and rebirth.

Before fading from view, Dion served two ruby-colored cocktails on a small silver tray, delicately placing one on each side table atop a white linen coaster. "The Potter Inquiry," he said, "London dry gin with cassis and a touch of Lillet Blanc." The drink gleamed like a jewel in the low light, crowned with a fresh mint leaf.

"Remember," Dion whispered, "some journeys divide us from what we've known, while others connect us to what we've forgotten. Your true self awaits in the spaces between." With those words, he seemed to blend into the room's ambient luster, not vanishing but becoming less distinct, as if Phoenix's perception of him was softening around the edges.

oooo

Alone momentarily, Phoenix exhaled fully, feeling his body sink deeper into the chair. The beam from above intensified, casting the room in a glow between twilight and dawn. Time seemed suspended, as if the cadence of his heartbeat had replaced the usual progress of seconds.

He sipped the cocktail, its complexity opening further on his palate with each taste. The comfort it generated spread through his limbs, loosening the habitual pressure in his torso. Prudence's likely reaction to this place flashed through his mind—her inevitable recoil from its sensuality, ambiguity, and threat to her carefully ordered worldview.

Her father's voice evident in her responses to anything that challenged convention. "This is what happens when people stray from scripture," she would say, parroting the man whose approval she'd never won despite decades of trying.

Lilith—this room would enchant her, and she would likely sketch it furiously, trying to capture its unique dimensions and the feeling of existing outside of ordinary time. She would run her hands along the bookshelves, exclaiming over each rare volume, connecting it to some obscure philosophical concept he'd only half-understand.

Body tingling, Phoenix was aware of each breath, heartbeat, and sensation of muscle and bone. He was determined to absorb every moment of this experience—an unexpected gift.

His gaze drifted around the circular room again, taking in its impossible treasures—the four paintings oscillated gently in the starry shine, their images deepening with continued observation. The books on the shelves stood like sentinels, millennia of human thought and imagination bound in leather, cloth, and papyrus.

The four books he had chosen—or that had chosen him—waited on the table beside him. Four volumes, four essentials that he had denied himself: curiosity, sensuality, emotional truth, and spiritual freedom.

oooo

As Phoenix settled deeper into the chair, absorbing the impossible wonders of Mircea's inner sanctum, Dion returned with that fluid grace that seemed to defy ordinary movement. The young man's eyes held a conspiratorial gleam.

"Before your first guide arrives," Dion said, his melodious voice pitched low as if sharing a cherished secret, "Mircea and I have something for you."

Dion moved to a section of shelving that Phoenix hadn't looked at before. With deliberate care, he withdrew a book, unlike the others. Even from a distance,

Phoenix could see this extraordinary volume, bound in rich burgundy leather, with intricate tooling adorning its cover.

"This is our gift to you," Dion said, standing before Phoenix. He presented the book with a slight bow as if offering something far more significant than paper and binding.

Accepting it, Phoenix was struck by its substantial weight. The leather felt impossibly smooth beneath his fingers, as if it had been handled for centuries yet remained perfectly preserved. Gold leaf embossing caught the light as he tilted the cover to read its title: *The Purging Room*.

"Open it," Dion encouraged, his expression of delighted anticipation.

Phoenix did, expecting to find printed text or perhaps elaborate illustrations. Instead, he discovered handmade paper the color of aged parchment, with a texture that spoke of artisanal craft. The pages appeared empty at first glance—until he looked more closely.

There, words appeared on the page in elegant calligraphy that seemed to materialize before his eyes. He blinked, sure he was imagining it, yet the phenomenon continued—an invisible handwriting with perfect penmanship, recording in real-time.

He looked up at Dion in astonishment and then returned to the page where the narrative continued, describing his wonderment.

"What is this?" Phoenix whispered, watching words form that transcribed his whispered question even as he spoke it.

"A chronicle," Dion replied, his eyes sparkling. "This book has recorded everything that has transpired since you entered our threshold—your conversations, experiences, thoughts—all inscribed as they happen."

Phoenix turned pages backward, finding earlier encounters documented in the same meticulous script. His arrival at the unmarked door, his first meeting with Dion, and Mircea's recognition in the speakeasy.

"But how—"

"The 'how' matters less than the 'why,'" Dion interrupted gently. "This record will continue to write itself long after you depart our threshold. Your story—the one beginning tonight—will unfold in these pages as you live it."

Phoenix ran his fingertips over the words, feeling a slight impression of the letters as if they were still settling into the paper. "This is impossible," he murmured.

"No more impossible than transformation itself," Dion replied. "No more miraculous than the constant authoring of our lives through choice and attention."

The magnitude of this gift slowly dawned on Phoenix —not merely a record of tonight's experiences but a continuing account of whatever path emerged from this pivotal encounter. The implications were dizzying.

"Each of your guides will have this volume while you converse," Dion explained, extending his hands to reclaim the book temporarily. "It would be too distracting to see your experiences recorded as you live them. We want you to be fully present. At the conclusion of your journey here, Mircea and I will return it to you before your departure."

Phoenix reluctantly surrendered the book, observing Dion placing it on the side table of the opposite leather chair and tenderly closing it.

"Now," Dion said, moving toward the door, "your first guide awaits. Remember—everything that unfolds here is already becoming part of your story, whether recorded in mystical ink or the deeper inscriptions of your understanding."

oooo

Phoenix reached for the first book on his side table, *The Tale of Peter Rabbit by H.B.P.*, with a simple gray paper cover and black lettering. A wave of nostalgia swept over him—he hadn't thought of this children's story since reading it to his daughters when they were small.

Tracing the lettering before opening the cover, he saw it was modest in appearance—about five inches square, with just 41 pages. He smiled at the black-and-white line illustrations, remembering how Faith and Judith had giggled at the mischievous rabbit's adventures. However, he faintly remembered color images in their family copy.

Absorbed in these unexpected memories, Phoenix didn't immediately notice something new in the room's surroundings, a movement in the illumination from above.

The constellations in the domed ceiling began rearranging, stars sliding across the celestial canvas with deliberate purpose rather than cosmic randomness. As Phoenix watched, transfixed, the stars formed what appeared to be a rectangular outline high above, filling the sky. Within this stellar frame, darkness deepened, creating a stark contrast against the surrounding heavens.

Then, with a gentle unfolding that defied physical logic, this rectangular darkness opened like an immense book—the same burgundy leather volume Dion had placed on the side table now manifested at colossal scale among the stars. Its massive pages spread across the dome, the gold-tooled edges gleaming like distant galaxies.

"Incredible," Phoenix whispered, his neck craned upward in wonder.

The celestial book's first pages were not blank. Elegant script unfurled across them in real-time, letters forming against the cream parchment background. With a start, Phoenix realized he was witnessing his own experience recorded in the vast book above. The narration continued to appear, describing his reaction to seeing it:

*"Incredible," Phoenix whispered, his neck craned upward in wonder.*

Feeling a strange sensation—a mixture of vertigo and déjà vu—Phoenix twitched in his chair. The movement was immediately captured in the cosmic text:

*Feeling a strange sensation—a mixture of vertigo and
déjà vu—Phoenix twitched in his chair.*

A chill ran through him as he grasped the abnormal reality of watching his experiences transcribed mere moments after they occurred, as if some omniscient author were documenting his journey perfectly. The book wasn't just recording events but seemingly capturing his thoughts.

"Who is writing this?" he asked aloud, partly to test the book and partly out of genuine bewilderment.

As Phoenix waited, the celestial pages began to turn of their own accord, the massive movement creating gentle currents of air that stirred his hair. Each new page revealed different moments from his time in the Purging Room—the absinthe drink, his conversation with Mircea, the presentation of the magical book itself.

The pages turned faster, creating a breeze sweeping through the circular room. Then they slowed, settling on a blank spread. Phoenix held his breath, watching as new words began to form:

*The enormous book began to fold inward, stars flowing
around its edges like cosmic bookmarks. The burgundy
cover closed emphatically, then began to shrink. As it
diminished in size, it also descended, floating downward with dreamlike grace.*

The book continued to transform as it hovered downward, its shape wavering and morphing. By the time it reached the midpoint, it was changing rapidly—the leather binding elongating in some places, contracting in others. Colors changed, textures transformed, until what settled into the opposite chair was no longer a book but a refined and venerable woman.

She held the original burgundy volume in her hands, now returned to its proper size. Briefly regarding Phoenix, she looked inside it, nodded approvingly, and then decorously placed it closed on her side table.

"Well," she said, her refined London accent breaking the spell of silence, "I see you've had an awakening of sorts."

# CHAPTER FIVE

## Curious Mind

There was something new in the room's environment—a faint scent of lavender and garden soil, the soft rustle of wool against leather. Then, that formal voice helped pull him together.

"Well," the woman said, sounding both polished and amused, "I see you've found my little book."

Phoenix straightened in his chair, feeling oddly like a schoolboy caught daydreaming by a favorite teacher.

"You're Beatrix Potter," he said, surprise evident. "It's nice to meet you. I'm Phoenix Adams." Standing, he offered a hand, "It's an honor to meet you, Ms. Potter. I didn't expect ... well, any of this, really."

"Indeed. I know who you are." Taking his hand, she inclined her head, the tilting thoughtful and economical.

"You're a man who has spent decades closing doors rather than opening them. Rather like Peter Rabbit's sisters, who choose the safety of home over the adventure of the garden."

"Please, do relax," Potter said, waving away his discomfort briskly. "Children's stories often contain the truths we most need to remember as adults, don't they?"

Her gray hair was arranged in a neat bun at the nape of her neck. She wore a high-necked dress of slate blue wool, its severe cut softened by a cameo brooch at her collar. Though outwardly prim, her eyes sparkled with unmistakable intelligence and barely suppressed mischief. Her mouth, seemingly set in a disapproving line, twitched at one corner as if perpetually about to share a clever observation.

Laugh lines radiated from her eyes, evidence of a life filled with genuine amusement. Yet, she did not seem one for meaningless chit-chat.

"Now then," Potter continued, settling more comfortably in her chair and arranging her skirt with practiced efficiency. "We have matters of the mind to discuss, questions of curiosity and intellectual courage." She pronounced each word with careful emphasis that suggested its importance.

"Oh my," she exclaimed, seeing the ruby cocktail on the table beside her and tasting it. It was dry London gin with a hint of sweetness. You have one as well. That delightful scapegrace Dion named this after me. And look, he garnished it with a fresh mint leaf. Perfect."

"You're not what I expected," he declared.

"Few interesting things ever are," she replied, her expression softening. "That's the point of our conversation, Mr. Adams. Expectations are the enemies of discovery." She returned her drink to the side table, dabbing the corner of her mouth with a handkerchief. "One must approach the world with one's eyes properly open, not half-closed by what one presumes to find."

As she spoke, the room's atmosphere changed. The air seemed to vibrate with energy—the anticipation of discovery, of unknown doors waiting to be opened.

"Tell me, when did you stop asking questions?" Potter asked, folding her hands in her lap. Her posture was impeccably proper yet conveyed genuine interest.

The query was unexpected, and his response emerged unfiltered: "What do you mean?"

"There," she said, pointing at him like a naturalist who had spotted a rare specimen, "that's more like it. A question in response to a question. The natural state of the human mind is curiosity, Mr. Adams. Children understand this instinctively. They question everything, examine everything, imagine everything."

Her eyes narrowed, "Until they're taught not to."

Fidgeting in his chair, a clench formed in his jaw. "I ask plenty of questions. I'm a businessman. It's part of the job."

"Yes," she sat up a bit straighter, "but those are sanctioned questions, aren't they? Perfectly proper inquiries within the confines of what's deemed appropriate for a man in your position." She patted her lap. "When did you last ask a question that frightened you? One that might lead to an answer you're unprepared to hear?"

Feeling his mouth dry, he reached for the cocktail beside him, buying himself time. The drink was perfect—intense but not bitter, with enough sweetness to smooth its edges.

"Or may I ask when you learned that questions were dangerous?" Beatrix asked, perching more deliberately at the edge of her seat.

oooo

The question triggered a disturbing memory. Phoenix was nine years old, sitting at the kitchen table, homework spread before him. He was working through his science textbook about dinosaurs and the age of the earth, fascinated by the colorful illustrations of prehistoric creatures and the timeline showing millions of years of evolution.

His father glanced over his shoulder, his face darkening as he saw the page. "That's not what the Bible teaches," he said, tight with disapproval.

"But which is true?" Phoenix had asked, genuinely confused. "The textbook or the Bible? They can't both be right, can they?"

His father's hand came down hard on the table, making the pencils jump. "We don't question God's word in this house," he'd said, low and threatening. "That's how doubt creeps in. That's how faith is destroyed."

The textbook disappeared the next day. When Phoenix asked about it, his mother said, "Your father demanded that your teacher find lessons more appropriate for you to study."

oooo

Blinking, he returned to the present moment, the memory's emotional weight still palpable. "I was nine," he said, the memory surprisingly straightforward after all these years. "A science textbook contradicted the Bible. When I asked about it, I learned that questions themselves were a betrayal."

"And what happened to your curiosity?" Beatrix prompted, her face showing a mixture of sympathy and indignation.

"It went underground," Phoenix disclosed. "I learned to compartmentalize. To ask certain questions in certain contexts. Science at school, faith at home and church. Never the twain shall meet."

"Oh my, the great bifurcation," Beatrix sighed. "The tragic splitting of knowledge into safe and dangerous categories. Rather like having a garden where certain plants are permitted, and others must be ruthlessly weeded out, regardless of their beauty or utility. And at church?" she continued. "I imagine your inquiring mind didn't always stay within the prescribed barriers there, either."

oooo

Her words conjured another memory: Phoenix, at eighteen, raised his hand during the college Bible study. The discussion had been about predestination and free will, and the speaker's neat explanations hadn't satisfied him.

"But if God knows everything in advance," he'd asked, "how can we have free will? And if we don't have free will, how can we be held responsible for our sins?"

The campus pastor's face had hardened. "Pride comes before a fall, Phoenix," he'd said, carrying a warning. "Smarter men than you have resolved these questions. Focus on obedience, not understanding."

He remembered how the other students had inched away from him as if doubt might be contagious. After the session, one of the seniors took him aside and suggested that he "pray for humility" when such questions arose.

oooo

Phoenix met Beatrix's understanding gaze, finding it easier to share with her than he'd expected. "I learned that curiosity was a form of pride," he said, the words becoming more manageable now. "That obedience was more important than understanding. That certain paradoxes weren't meant to be resolved but accepted."

"What a dreadful way to cage a young mind," Beatrix said with gentle indignation. "Like clipping a bird's wings and then wondering why it won't fly."

oooo

Her metaphor stirred a more recent and, in some ways, more painful memory: Five years ago, at a church leadership retreat, he'd been reading a book on Christian history that discussed the political factors influencing texts in the biblical canon. The senior pastor noticed the book and asked about it. When Phoenix shared some of the historical context he was learning, Rev. Edward's expression got concerned.

"Brother," he'd said, placing a firm hand on Phoenix's shoulder, "these academic approaches can be dangerous. They make us trust human wisdom over divine revelation. I'd be careful with material like this."

That night, Phoenix had hidden the book at the bottom of his suitcase. He'd finished it secretly, on a plane, where neither his wife nor his church colleagues would see it.

oooo

He absently traced the rim of his glass, the shame of that moment still fresh despite the years between. "Five years ago," he said, "I was reading about the historical formation of the Bible. The senior pastor warned me about 'academic approaches' to faith." He smiled sadly. "I finished the book secretly, like a teenager with contraband."

"And how did that feel?" Beatrix asked, her eyes keen. "This need to hide your intellectual exploration?"

"Shameful," Phoenix revealed. "And frustrating. I wanted to discuss what I was learning and wrestle with the implications. But there was no one safe to talk to." He paused. "Except my friend Lilith, later."

"So your curiosity became a secret shame," Beatrix observed. "Hidden away like my rabbit Peter hiding his escapades from his mother."

The comparison made him grin despite the bitter memories. "I suppose so."

"Yet here you are," Beatrix pointed out. "Which suggests some part of you has been nibbling at the edges of that forbidden garden all along."

Pondering this, Phoenix declared, "I've always had questions. They never really went away. I just learned to ignore them, to push them aside when they threatened to disrupt the life I'd built."

"The mind rebels against such constraints," Beatrix observed, noting Phoenix's slight frown. "Think of water, Mr. Adams. Even when we think we've locked all the doors—"

"Curiosity finds the cracks," Phoenix completed, understanding dawning.

"And seeps through," she finished with satisfaction. "Precisely."

"Is it really that simple?" Phoenix asked with genuine uncertainty. "Just ... allow myself to question again?"

"Oh, certainly not simple," Beatrix replied with a slight chuckle. "Decades of conditioning won't dissolve overnight. Those voices warning of danger and pride will continue to speak. The difference is whether you treat them as authoritative or as one perspective among many."

She sat straighter and sipped her libation, her expression serious momentarily. "Start with a single question that's been hovering at the edges of your mind—one that's been patiently waiting for your attention. Give it room. Explore it without demanding immediate answers. See where it leads."

He felt apprehension and then a hint of excitement rise in him. "I'm not sure I know how to do that anymore. I've spent my life focusing on what's useful," he said, the words sounding empty.

"Useful," she repeated, investing the word with gentle skepticism. "According to whom?"

Again, the question penetrated his defenses with surprising ease. According to whom, indeed?

"Your business world," Potter continued, "has taught you that knowledge is valuable only when it can be monetized. Curiosity becomes permissible only when it leads to patents, profits, or competitive advantage." She shook her head, those keen eyes showing a flash of indignation. "They've convinced you that wonder must justify itself through utility—that exploration without guaranteed returns is wasteful."

Shifting uncomfortably, he instinctively retorted, "Business demands efficiency."

"And destroys wonder in the process," Potter countered. "Look at how children explore—following questions simply because they arise, delighting in discovery for its own sake. Your economic system has no mechanism to value this kind of knowledge-seeking. It demands that curiosity be channeled exclusively toward what can be owned, packaged, and sold."

"Your job," Potter continued, her sharp eyes studying him, "has methods of stifling curiosity, hasn't it? Quite different from religious prohibition but no less effective." She savored another taste of her cocktail.

Memories from a product development meeting three years earlier surfaced. The conference room with its glass walls and polished table. His team discussing a new service offering.

"I once asked in a strategy meeting whether our new financial product might have negative consequences for certain communities," he told Potter. "The response was immediate—'That's not a P&L question.'"

"P&L?" she inquired, eyebrows raised.

"Profit and loss," he explained. "The CFO added that 'ethical considerations are for the compliance department, not the revenue meeting.' The message was clear—curiosity had its proper channels, and deviation wasn't welcome."

"And this question? Did you pursue it elsewhere?" Potter asked, adjusting her cameo brooch.

He shook his head. "I convinced myself it wasn't my department. The product launched, and two years later we faced backlash when its predatory aspects became public. I had sensed the problem but allowed my question to be contained."

"Categorization as a means of control," Potter observed. "Quite effective at keeping one's mind in acceptable corrals. Schools do it with subjects, churches with doctrine, and businesses with departments."

"The irony is that we claim to value innovation," he added. "Every corporate retreat has 'think outside the box' on banners, but actual boundary-crossing questions are treated like disruptions to efficiency."

"Yet the most valuable questions often reside at these intersections," Potter replied, tapping her finger once against the side of her glass. "In the wild spaces between your neat categorical gardens."

"The capacity for questioning never leaves us," Beatrix assured him. "Like Peter Rabbit's instinct to explore the garden despite all warnings to the contrary. It remains part of who we are, even when unused."

She pointed to the book in Phoenix's lap. "That's why children's stories endure, you know. They remind adults of what we once knew—curiosity is not a sin but a pathway to discovery. They tell us that questions aren't dangerous in themselves; only in the challenges they sometimes pose to established power."

Reality changed within him—not dramatically—but the first stirring of another long-dormant part of himself. "I could try," he said tentatively. "To ask one question. To see where it leads."

"That," Beatrix said with evident satisfaction, "is how the journey begins, not with grand declarations, but with the simple permission to wonder. Do you know another thing that saved me, Mr. Adams?" she continued, setting her glass down with a soft clink.

He shook his head.

"I was never sent to school." The statement carried a quiet pride. "My parents educated me at home, which meant I avoided having the curiosity systematically beaten out of me like many of my contemporaries. Dreadful institutions, most schools—designed to produce conformity rather than insight."

She reached beside her chair and produced a small leather portfolio, which she opened to reveal a series of watercolor paintings—exquisitely rendered rabbits, hedgehogs, mice, and other creatures, all engaged in surprisingly human activities."My family expected me to become an ornament in someone's parlor—to marry, produce children, and maintain a respectable home." She spoke matter-of-factly, but Phoenix detected an undercurrent of old rebellion.

"Instead, I spent my days observing rabbits in the garden, mice in the pantry, hedgehogs in the hedgerows." Her fingers caressed the paintings with evident affection. "I asked questions no proper Victorian lady was supposed to ask. How do animals behave when humans aren't watching? What stories might they tell about their lives? What if they wore waistcoats and carried umbrellas?" She glanced up with a conspiratorial wink. "Perfectly ridiculous questions by proper standards."

Phoenix was entranced, drawn in by the delicate beauty of her art and the passion in her voice.

"The questions seemed silly to others," she continued. "Childish. Beneath the dignity of a woman of my station. Yet they led me here." Her eyes focused on the book in Phoenix's lap with evident satisfaction. "To stories that have delighted generations of children. To be independent when women were expected to be dependent. To a life of my own making rather than one prescribed by others."

Her words struck a chord within Phoenix. The careful categories containing his life suddenly seemed arbitrary—professional, familial, religious, social—each with its rigid set of rules and expectations—borders he'd never dared cross.

"There is something delicious about writing the first words of a book," Potter said, her gaze distant now, focused on some beloved memory. "You never know where they'll take you. Rather like following a rabbit down a hole."

"I haven't written a story since grade school," Phoenix acknowledged, surprised by his wistfulness.

"You've lived one," Potter observed, her clear eyes fixing on him again. "A story—one with predictable chapters and a predetermined ending. The Successful Executive. The Family Man. The Church Elder." She tilted her head, "Are you enjoying this story you've been writing, Mr. Adams?"

The question penetrated deeper than he was prepared for. Phoenix's hand tightened around the delicate stem of his glass, fingers whitening with the pressure. "It's been a good life," he said automatically.

"I didn't ask if it was good. I asked if you were enjoying it." Potter's tone remained gentle despite the frankness of her words. "There's a difference, you know. Rather like the difference between eating a snack and having a proper feast."

He carefully set the glass down, noticing a slight shake in his fingers. "I've been..." he began, then stopped, searching for the right word. "Restless," he finally said.

"Ah, restlessness." Potter's face brightened with recognition. "The mind's way of telling us it's starved. When was the last time you fed yours, Mr. Adams? Not with spreadsheets, sermon points, or social obligations, but with genuine wonder? When did you last allow yourself the pleasure of a truly outrageous idea?"

Phoenix couldn't remember. With Lillith? His reading had been restricted to business books and approved religious texts, and he could barely recall what it looked like to read purely for pleasure. His travels had been reduced to the utilitarian interiors of cookie-cutter hotel rooms and conference centers that could have been anywhere in the world.

"I used to read everything I could get my hands on," he confessed. "Science fiction, philosophy, history—anything that offered a window into different ways of thinking."

"And now?" Potter prompted.

"Now I read what's useful," he said, his words sounding hollow even to himself.

"Useful," she repeated, investing the word with gentle skepticism. "According to whom? Who appointed these arbiters of what knowledge deserves your attention?"

Again, the question penetrated his defenses with surprising ease. According to whom, indeed? His church, which provided approved reading lists? His business partners, who valued pragmatism over exploration? His wife, who viewed his former intellectual curiosity and love of beauty as a potential threat?

"I have responsibilities," he said.

"As did I," Potter countered, straightening her impeccable posture. "To my family, society, to the expectations of my class and gender. Had I allowed those responsibilities to define the limits of my curiosity, my life would have been a fraction of what it became." She waved at the circular room around them.

"Look at these books, Mr. Adams. Each represents a question someone dared to ask despite the consequences. Frightfully impertinent questions, many of them."

His gaze traveled along the bookshelves lining the walls, taking in titles that spanned centuries and encompassed cultures. Some were familiar, but many more were unknown to him—evidence of how narrow his intellectual world had become.

"You're suggesting I should what? Abandon my faith? Turn my back on everything I've built?" Despite himself, an edge of defensiveness crept in his words.

Potter's laugh was surprisingly gracious. "Goodness, no. What a terribly American response—all extremes and absolutes." She took another taste from her glass. "I'm suggesting you might question it. Explore it. Test its perimeters and examine its foundations. Like a good gardener inspecting the soil before planting."

Her eyes narrowed. "True faith can withstand questioning, Mr. Adams. It's dogma that requires unthinking acceptance."

Her words echoed thoughts Phoenix had barely allowed himself to acknowledge. How often had he sat in church, listening to sermons that reduced the mysteries of existence to simplistic formulas and certainties? How often had he sensed the narrowness of the box into which his spiritual life had been packed?

"When I was a child," Potter continued, her voice softening with memory, "I half believed and wholly played with fairies. What heaven can be more real than to retain the spirit world of childhood, tempered and balanced by knowledge and common sense?" She gave him an impish grin. "Not quite the doctrine your American evangelists preach, I imagine."

"My church would say that's paganism," Phoenix observed, though without the certainty he would have expressed a day earlier.

"Your church says many things, I imagine," Potter replied, unperturbed, adjusting a stray pin in her bun. "As do all outward forms of religion. Yet most seem to cause endless strife, don't they? Rather like children fighting over who has the better imaginary friend." She sipped her cocktail thoughtfully. "I came to believe there is a great power at work in nature. Beyond that, it seemed most sensible to behave myself and never mind the rest. I found meaning and purpose through careful observation of the natural world rather than through religious institutions."

Smiling at her practical spiritual approach, he stated, "That's heresy according to my denomination."

"Heresy," Potter mused, rolling the word on her tongue like an exciting flavor. "From the Greek *hairesis*—meaning 'choice' or 'thing chosen.' How revealing that choosing for oneself is considered the gravest of sins." She tapped the table with one finger for emphasis. "Peter

Rabbit was a heretic too, you know. Choosing to enter the garden despite all warnings to the contrary. Frightfully disobedient creature."

"He nearly got caught and made into a pie," Phoenix pointed out with a wink, warming to the metaphor.

"Indeed," Potter agreed, her eyes sparkling. "There are always risks in questioning confines. But consider the alternative—never knowing what grows in that garden, never tasting those forbidden vegetables, never experiencing the thrill of outwitting Mr. McGregor."

She edged closer, her posture still impeccably proper. "Would it have been better for Peter to stay safely at home with his more obedient siblings? With Flopsy, Mopsy, and Cotton-tail, eating the bread and milk that Mother Rabbit provided?"

Weighing this, Phoenix replied, "I suppose not. Yet he did get into trouble."

"He did," Potter affirmed. "He came home, took the chamomile tea his mother offered, and went to bed wiser than before." She fixed Phoenix with a penetrating look. "The mistake is not in questioning, Mr. Adams. It's believing that questions lead only to trouble instead of enjoyment."

Again, Phoenix sensed a movement within his body, a loosening of constrictions he had carried so long that he'd forgotten they weren't natural. His breathing deepened as the pressure in his shoulders once again released."What if I don't like the answers I find?" he asked, voicing a fear that had lurked beneath his conformity for years.

"You'll have the satisfaction of discovering them for yourself instead of accepting them secondhand," Potter replied. "Rather like the difference between seeing a garden in a picture book and walking through it yourself, thorns, weeds and all."

She straightened an already immaculate cuff. "I suspect what truly frightens you is not disliking the answers but liking them too much—finding that the world is wider, more wondrous, and less rigidly ordered than you've been taught to believe."

Her perception was spot-on, and Phoenix experienced exposure, as if she could see directly into the chambers of his mind. He had a sudden, visual memory of sitting in a college philosophy class, encountering ideas that both thrilled and terrified him with their implications—but then swiftly retreating into the safety of unquestioning beliefs.

"I wanted to be a writer once," he admitted. The confession emerged from some long-buried part of himself. "To explore ideas through fiction. My father said it wasn't a proper career for a man with my potential."

Potter's expression softened. "You set aside that curiosity, that creative impulse, to follow a more approved path." It wasn't a question but a statement of recognition.

"Do you know, Mr. Adams, I was nearly forty years old before I published my first book? Until then, I had dutifully repressed my true interests in favor of acting the proper daughter."

"What changed?" Phoenix asked, genuinely curious now.

"I grew tired of living someone else's idea of my life," she said. "I realized that time was passing whether or not I pursued my curiosities." She lovingly touched the paintings beside her. "These little watercolors were for me at first. Private pleasures. Eventually, I understood that keeping them to myself was a waste."

He reflected on his secret inner world—the questions he had learned to keep to himself, the doubts he had buried beneath layers of certainty. What might emerge if he gave them air and illumination?

"Your curiosity hasn't died, Mr. Adams," Potter said as if reading his thoughts. "It's merely been channeled into safe, approved directions. Like a river forced into canals instead of allowed to find its natural course."

Phoenix frowned, absently tracing a pattern on the arm of his chair. "But how do I undo decades of ... channeling?" The word felt inadequate for the systematic narrowing of his mind.

She took another studied sip of her drink, eyes watching him over the rim of her glass. "The questions you've never dared ask still live within you, waiting for permission to emerge."

"Where would I even begin?" His voice carried a note of genuine uncertainty.

"Begin anywhere," Potter replied with a look that transformed her prim features. She set her glass down with deliberate care. "That's the beauty of curiosity—one question leads naturally to the next."

Phoenix glanced at the countless books lining the circular room, each representing a path of inquiry he had denied himself. The sheer possibility was overwhelming.

"It's important to follow where they lead," she continued, noting his hesitation, "even when—especially when—they take you beyond the fences you've accepted as uncrossable." She leaned back, a mischievous glint in her eye. "Rather like following a rabbit hole to see where it might lead."

She reached across and deftly took the book from his lap, opening it to an illustration of Peter Rabbit squeezing under Mr. McGregor's garden gate.

"Look at his eyes," she said, pointing to the image. "That's not only mischief you see there. It's wonder. The recognition that a world of new experiences, tastes, dangers, and discoveries lies beyond this fence." Her finger traced the illustration with evident affection. "We're born with that look, Mr. Adams. Some of us manage to keep it. Others have been educated, disciplined, or frightened out of them. Properly tamed, as it were."

Phoenix studied the image, seeing for the first time the complexity beneath its apparent simplicity. The rabbit's expression contained a mixture of trepidation and irrepressible curiosity that resonated deeply with his current state. "I have questions," he said quietly. "About everything. My faith, my marriage, my work ... even myself. Things I've never allowed myself to examine too closely."

"Yes, certainly you have questions," Potter said, her voice gentle but matter-of-fact. "You're human. Curiosity is a birthright, just as fundamental as the physical pleasures your church has taught you to deny." A hint of playfulness returned to her expression. "I suspect you'll find the two are more closely related than your religion has led you to believe."

Questions rose to Phoenix's face at the implication, but he nodded in agreement.

"The mind hungers for exploration as the body hungers for touch," Potter continued. "Deny either desire long enough, and important parts of yourself begin to wither." She placed the book on the table. "You've begun to reclaim one aspect of your nature. Soon, you'll have the opportunity to explore another." She flashed a coy wink.

Phoenix's face grew reflective, feeling the truth of her words resound within him. How long had it been since he had pursued a question simply for the joy of discovery? Since he had read a book that wasn't pre-approved or professionally useful? Since he had allowed his mind to wander beyond the carefully demarcated territories of truth that had been programmed into him?

"There is courage in curiosity," Potter observed. "A willingness to risk certainty for the possibility of wonder." She chuckled, the expression transforming her prim features into girlishness. "It took me over seventy years to discover all the questions I might have asked. You're—what? Forty-seven? You have time yet if you're brave enough to use it."

The observation struck Phoenix with unexpected force. He did have time—hopefully, decades—but only if he chose to use it differently than the years already behind him."I'm fearful," the confession cost him less than he might have expected.

"Good," Potter said with surprising firmness. "Fear means you're considering possibilities beyond the safe and familiar. Fear is often the gatekeeper to the most rewarding discoveries." She straightened her skirt with deliberate hands. "The question is not whether you're fearful, Mr. Adams, but whether you'll allow that fear to determine the margins of your life."

A craving began to develop within Phoenix—to know, understand, and explore the questions he had carefully avoided for decades."I don't know where to start," he said honestly.

"Start with a question hovering at the edges of your mind," Potter suggested. "One you've been too afraid or too busy to examine. Give it your full attention. See where it leads you." Her face lit up with genuine enthusiasm. "To put it differently, there is something delicious about the first question of an inquiry. You never know where it will take you."

As she spoke, he noticed that her form had begun to shimmer, becoming less substantial.

"Our time grows short," Potter said, seemingly untroubled by her increasing transparency. "Remember this: curiosity is not childish, Mr. Adams. It is one of the most profoundly adult qualities we can cultivate—the willingness to remain unfinished, to allow our understanding to evolve, to approach the world with wonder rather than certainty."

She adjusted her brooch one final time. "Dreadfully important, that."

Wanting to thank her and ask more questions, he was overcome by an unusual fatigue. His eyelids were weighted, and it was challenging to keep them open despite his desire to prolong this fascinating conversation.

"Rest now," Potter's voice came to him as if from a growing distance. "Dream of questions, not answers. Answers close doors. Questions open them. Rather like the difference between a locked garden gate and one left ajar. Curious minds are never truly alone, Mr. Adams. They're always accompanied by the questions that illumine their way forward."

She left behind only the faint scent of cassis, earthy gardens, and a hunger for discovery that Phoenix could already feel taking root within him.

oooo

Phoenix closed his jet-lagged eyes, feeling sleep overtake him. Instead, a gentle sound caught his attention—the delicate rustling of pages turning. The noise grew and multiplied until a hundred invisible hands seemed to be leafing through books around him.

The sound transformed, becoming melodic—each page turn contributing a distinct note to an otherworldly composition. High, fluttering tones from what might be ancient papyrus; low, resonant notes from leather-bound volumes; crisp, precise sounds from modern pages. Together, they created a haunting bibliophonic orchestra to celebrate the written word.

Phoenix opened his eyes to witness a fantastic sight. Books had opened of their own accord throughout the circular room, their pages turning in perfect synchronism. Some released tiny motes of golden light that drifted upward like luminescent pollen. Others seemed to whisper fragments of stories in voices just below the threshold of comprehension. The ambiance was charged with narrative possibility.

Near the ceiling, the pages from dozens of books appeared to have detached, forming a slowly rotating vortex of text and illustration. As Phoenix watched, transfixed, the pages began to dance more deliberately, folding and refolding themselves like literary origami. They created shapes—a rabbit, a rose, a mask, a Celtic spiral—each holding form for moments before dissolving and reforming.

The rustling intensified, creating a crescendo of paper music that seemed to vibrate in his ears and throughout his entire body. The vortex of pages spiraled downward, encircling him in a gentle whirlwind of words and images. As they spun, Phoenix caught glimpses of illustrations—watercolor landscapes, a sinuous curve, a face exhibiting joy, and a scenic lake—each visible momentarily before replaced by another.

Then, with a sound like a collective sigh, the pages settled. The room returned to stillness, but the air remained charged with a different quality than before—

more sensual, more physical, as if the room had transfigured from the imaginative to the bodily.

# CHAPTER SIX

## Body and Desire

The gentle starlight returned and was soothing. Two new amber-colored cocktails were on each side table in crystal coupe glasses with faceted stems and garnished with Luxardo cherries. Mysteriously refreshed and curious, he picked one up, and the aromas enveloped his senses. Rich tobacco, leather, and cocoa scents hinted at an exquisite aged Cognac. Almost tasting it, he hesitated, intuition telling him to wait before drinking. Carefully placing it back on the side table, he picked up the next book, *The Story of O* (*Histoire d'O*).

Its pages were yellowed with age, the plain cream cover listing only the title and the pseudonym Pauline Réage. Turning to the flip side of the cover page, he noted the publisher, Jean-Jacques Pauvert, and the date 1954. It had vintage typography reminiscent of another time. There was no provocative imagery to indicate the highly controversial content.

It was a book he had heard whispered about but never dared seek out, representing everything his church had condemned as sinful and corrupting. His fingers trembled as he opened to the beginning. The paper sighed softly, like breath released after being held too long. Inexplicably, Phoenix read the French words unfurling before him in perfect comprehensibility despite his limited language knowledge.

The text immediately enthralled him, and he didn't notice the new aromas or the soft sound of fabric moving against skin. The perfume was a blend of jasmine and roses with the faintest hint of vanilla. Then, a voice—female, tinged with a French accent—took his attention from the page.

"It takes courage to truly look at desire, doesn't it?"

Phoenix's head jerked up, his spine straightening in shock. The book nearly slipped from his nerveless fingers. The woman's dark eyes held his with knowing intensity. She held his chronicle in one delicate hand.

"Pauline Réage," she said, extending the other hand, "though that is not my true name, as I'm sure you know. We have much to discuss about what you've denied yourself, Phoenix Adams."

He hesitated only briefly before standing and reaching to take her hand, "Ms. Réage."

"Indeed, *enchanté*, please call me Pauline," she smiled, her eyes showing warmth. "Just as that sweetheart Beatrix helped you start questioning the cage around your mind, I'm here to help you examine the one you've built around your body." She settled into the blue leather chair across from him and placed his burgundy book beside her drink on the side table.

"*À la découverte*," she said, gracefully raising her glass, "to discovery—of pleasures long denied and truths long buried." After raising her glass to toast, Pauline took a first sip. Her eyelids fluttered closed momentarily, her full lips parting as the flavors spread across her palate.

A soft, almost imperceptible sigh escaped her throat before her eyes opened again, now gleaming with heightened pleasure. "*Bon sang!*" she exclaimed in a hushed, intimate tone, one hand rising unconsciously to her mouth. "*C'est jouissif!*—It's exhilarating!" After drinking liberally, she opened Phoenix's book and tittered as it recorded her exclamation about the drink.

Where Potter had been all prim propriety and hidden mischief, this woman presented a study in sensual openness. Her dark hair fell in loose waves, framing a face of classic Mediterranean beauty. She wore a dress of sheer silken material bordering on transparency, clinging to her voluptuous curves like a second skin.

High cheekbones highlighted eyes that projected allure, strength, and empathy. Her full lips curved into a caring smile that seemed to know him already better than he knew himself. Tiny lines radiated from the corners of her eyes, evidence of a life of intense expression. Her skin held the soft glow of the Mediterranean sun, and a single lock of curly dark hair fell across her forehead in deliberate disarray.

She had a face and body that might have belonged to Monica Bellucci's French cousin—sensual but somehow less intimidating in beauty. Her face invited confidence instead of creating distance.

Phoenix straightened involuntarily, feeling a totally different awareness than he had with Ms. Potter. Her stunning aura made him feel trepidation, and her voluptuousness was impossible to dismiss.

"You're afraid," she said, her accent caressing the English words like velvet, "not of me, *mon cher*, but of what I represent." She knowingly repositioned her lush body, the fabric of her dress whispering against her skin.

Phoenix cleared his throat, struggling to find his executive voice, the one that commanded boardrooms and closed multi-million dollar deals. "I'm not afraid," he managed, the denial artificial.

She leaned in, causing her dress to shift, revealing more of her soft and full breasts. "Your body disagrees with your denial," she said, nodding toward his trembling hands. "It's always wiser than our minds, you know. *Plus honnête.* More honest."

"Ah, but curiosity has already begun to open doors within you, has it not?" she said, an empathic smile on her lips. "Ms. Potter has awakened your questioning mind. Be warned, she has taught me to ask many questions as well. They may seem uncomfortable at first, *chéri*, but please humor me. Now it is time to question what you've been taught about your body."

He placed her book on the side table as if creating distance from its contents might protect him. "How are you here?" he asked, "You can't be ... real."

A knowing laugh escaped her, rich and abandoned, "*Ma foi.* I'm as palpable as Beatrix. Does it matter? Reality is simply what we agree to experience together." She made an elegant wave that commanded the chamber around them. "Is any of this 'real' by your everyday standards? Yet you feel it, *non?* The weight of the books, the taste of the cocktails, the racing of your pulse when you first saw me."

Phoenix couldn't dispute that. Every stimulus in this room came across as more delineated, more real than the life he had built for himself. He looked down at the book he had set aside.

"You know my work," she said, following his gaze, "or you know *of* it. The forbidden book whispered about but rarely read."

"*The Story of O* follows a beautiful Parisian fashion photographer who willingly submits herself to a series of increasingly intense sexual experiences at a chateau called Roissy. There, she surrenders control completely, becoming 'O' - a symbol of her abandonment of identity and autonomy. The novel explores how O's submission paradoxically becomes her path to freedom and how surrendering control leads to self-discovery."

"It's not mere titillation, Phoenix. It examines desire, power, identity, and the complex relationship between submission and autonomy—themes your church has likely never allowed you to explore honestly."

She looked at him directly, "Just as your mind has hungered for questions, has your body not hungered for authentic experience? The curiosity Beatrix awakened need not stop at the neck, you know. Be honest. Has denying your physical desires led to fulfillment?"

The question landed like a stone in still water, sending ripples through Phoenix's consciousness. With Beatrix, he had begun to question intellectual constraints; now Pauline invited him to extend that questioning to his physical self.

As he took a sip of his drink to avoid answering immediately, memories surfaced unbidden—years of rigid self-control, of pleasures denied then sought in secret corners of his life, always followed by waves of shame that threatened to drown him.

Pauline seemed content to wait in the silence.

"I'm a church elder, one of the dozen men who lead the congregation alongside the pastor," he finally said, "I have responsibilities."

"To whom? To what?" Her eyes held his, refusing to release him into evasion. She smiled, a determined glint in her eye. "What about your responsibility to yourself? To the hunger that has begun to devour you from within?" She traced a finger along the rim of her glass. "You Americans, always putting duty before pleasure as if they were enemies rather than lovers."

An unfamiliar perception emerged—as if rules long calcified in his body had begun to soften, just as his mind had started to unlock under Beatrix's guidance. "I was taught that certain ... desires ... are sinful. That they lead to destruction."

"Again, has denying them led to fulfillment?" her question contained no judgment, only genuine curiosity, much like Beatrix's queries about his intellectual constraints. She tilted her head, studying him with those discerning eyes.

The question pierced Phoenix with its accuracy. How long had it been since Prudence had aroused him? Years, at least. Their bedroom had become a battleground where his desire was treated as evidence of his depravity.

"No," he admitted softly, "denying them has not led to fulfillment." Phoenix hesitated, the question penetrating deeper. "I was taught early that the body is dangerous," he said. "That it needs to be controlled."

"When, *mon cher?*" Pauline asked softly. "When did you first learn to fear your body rather than celebrate it?"

oooo

His mind drifted unexpectedly to a summer day when he was eleven. The church youth group had gone swimming at the lake. He'd been racing with friends, delighting in the cool water against his skin after hours in the sun, the physical joy of jostling and competition.

Pastor Williams had pulled him aside, his expression serious. "A godly boy covers himself," he said, handing him a t-shirt to wrap around his swimming trunks. "Modesty isn't just for the girls, Phoenix."

He remembered the confusion and shame that had washed over him, the sudden awareness of his obvious arousal as dangerous, a sin that needed to be hidden. The other boys had snickered, and he'd worn the shirt for the remainder of the outing, soggy and uncomfortable but "appropriate."

oooo

The memory was so fresh that he found himself sharing it aloud. "I was eleven," Phoenix said quietly. "It was a church outing at the lake. I was swimming with friends, and the pastor told me I needed to cover up. That modesty wasn't just for girls."

Pauline sighed, genuine sadness in her expression. "The shaming begins so early, *non*? The child, innocent in his body, taught that this body part—this magnificent creation—is somehow obscene." She leaned closer. "And later? When did desire become sinful?"

oooo

Another memory surfaced—youth camp at sixteen, the guest speaker pacing across the stage with intense energy, words rising and falling dramatically as he described the dangers of lust. "Male desire is like a beast that must be tamed," the man had thundered, pounding the podium for emphasis. "Every lustful look at a woman is fornication in your heart."

Phoenix had walked out of that session feeling mutilated, as though his longings had been severed. The following week, he'd thrown away the art and photography magazines he'd collected, with their nudes he'd found so beautiful, afraid they were evidence of his depravity. He'd prayed for hours, begging God to take away the "beast" of his desire.

oooo

"They compared desire to a beast," Phoenix told Pauline, speaking low. "A wild thing that needed to be caged."

"And so you built the cage," Pauline observed gently, "bar by bar, year by year, until you could no longer reach what was imprisoned inside."

He nodded slowly, the metaphor echoing within. "There was another incident," he said, the memory rising unbidden. "In college. I was twenty. I'd met a girl in my literature class. We'd been dating for a few months, and things were becoming ... physical." He fell silent, the memory still painful after all these years.

"What happened?" Pauline prompted softly.

"Her father was a member at my church," Phoenix continued. "He found out and called my parents. They called my pastor and scheduled a 'restoration session.' Three hours of lectures saying that I was leading her toward sin, that my physical desires were corrupting her." He swallowed hard. "They made me grovel at their feet and pray and confess my 'impurity.'"

"*Mon Dieu*," Pauline whispered, "such cruelty in the name of holiness."

"We broke up the next day," he finished. "She couldn't bear the shame. I couldn't either. I threw myself into Bible studies and accountability groups—weekly meetings where men confessed struggles and kept each other in line. I started dating Prudence six months later—the pastor's daughter. The 'safe' choice."

"And your desire?" Pauline asked, "What happened to it?"

"I buried it," Phoenix said. "Or thought I did. I focused on acceptable goals—career, church leadership, and family. But it never really went away. It just went underground. Finding an outlet in ways I had been taught was shameful. Glimpses of films. Forbidden books and magazines. Masturbation. Fantasies. Eventually, Lilith." He paused. "But always with a layer of shame and guilt attached."

"The body remembers what the mind tries to forget," Pauline said, touching his hand lightly. "These experiences—they did not just teach you ideas about desire, they inscribed them into your very skin, your muscles, your nerves. The stress you carry in your shoulders and how you hold your breath when speaking of these things are physical manifestations of the cage."

As if reading his mind, she asked, "When did your desire become shameful in your marriage?"

oooo

Vivid images of his marital bed flashed through his mind
—the mechanical, dutiful encounters with Prudence, her
face turned away, the routine they had established that
contained neither passion nor discovery—his furtive moments alone, always followed by self-recrimination. Then
Lilith appeared in his thoughts, their body and spirit
equally engaged, the first time he'd been truly alive in
decades.

oooo

He paused to take a drink. The memory was fresh despite
occurring some time ago: "It was 2000. We had just gotten our first home computer with internet access—a
bulky beige desktop that seemed miraculous then. Prudence had insisted it be kept in the kitchen so the girls'
online activities could be monitored."

He remembered the evening clearly—coming home
late from work to find Prudence sitting at the kitchen table, her face pale and tight with anger, the computer
screen glowing accusingly. "I had been researching classi-
cal art for a presentation, primarily Renaissance masters.
I'd bookmarked several museum sites and online
galleries."

He shook his head, "She found the bookmarks and
opened them. Sites with Botticelli's Venus, Michelangelo's David, and nudes I found aesthetically beautiful. She
called it pornography," he continued, "said I was 'feeding
my lust' with 'images of nakedness.' She'd called her father that same evening—and told him she'd discovered

my 'secret sin.' He advised her to maintain physical distance until I'd shown 'genuine repentance.'"

"And after that?" Pauline prompted gently.

"She arranged for us to meet with the church counselor. Three sessions of advising that my appreciation for the human form was a 'gateway to adultery.' They insisted I install filtering software on our computer—the kind churches recommended to parents. I had to provide Prudence with the password so she could monitor my online activity." He laughed bitterly, "The screech of dial-up internet and parental control software—the technologies that killed whatever intimacy remained in our marriage."

Pauline sniffed, a sound that was sympathetic but exasperated. "Your culture has taught you to fear pleasure, to distrust the body's beauty. To believe that sensuality is separate from spirituality, not an expression of it. This illustrates how your education, as Beatrix showed you, taught you to fear certain questions and ideas."

"Those institutions taught you that pleasure is dangerous," Pauline observed, "but your business world reinforced this in its own way, *non?*"

Phoenix considered this. "The corporate environment doesn't explicitly condemn pleasure, but it certainly regiments the body," he acknowledged. "I remember a leadership retreat in Tokyo where we were scheduled down to five-minute intervals. One executive was tracking our steps with a stopwatch, saying, 'inefficient movement is wasted capital.'"

He smiled ruefully. "When I paused at a cherry blossom tree—literally stopped for thirty seconds to look up at it—my COO asked if I was feeling ill."

"The disembodied executive," Pauline said, nodding. "Valued only from the neck up, with the body treated as an inconvenient transport system for the brain. Another kind of sensual regulation."

"Our company fitness program is the same way," Phoenix added. "Exercise is presented purely as productivity enhancement. Our wellness consultant actually said, 'Each minute in the gym adds two minutes to your career longevity.' Even self-care has to be justified through ROI—return on investment."

"And how has this shaped your relationship with physical pleasure?" Pauline asked.

"I compartmentalize," Phoenix admitted. "Productivity in one box, pleasure in another—never to meet. Even my affair with Lilith is carefully scheduled, optimized for minimum risk and maximum ... benefit." He winced at his choice of words.

"Efficiency and pleasure are not enemies," Pauline said gently. "The body knows this instinctively, even if your corporate mindset has forgotten."

She opened her book, "Do you know why I wrote this?"

Phoenix shook his head.

"To explore the paradox that sometimes we find freedom in surrender. That pleasure and pain are not opposites but companions. That our deepest selves are often revealed in moments of greatest vulnerability." She ran her fingers lightly over the pages as one might caress a lover. "O discovered herself through experiences your church would condemn without understanding."

"Is that what this is about?" he asked. "Teaching me that sexual freedom is good, religious restriction is bad? I've heard that argument before."

Pauline's laugh was lilting and genuine. "You Americans reduce everything to such simple opposition. Black and white, good and bad, Madonna and whore." She waved a dismissive hand. "*Non*, Phoenix. This isn't about replacing one dogma with another." She moved toward him again. "It's about restoration. About reclaiming the parts of yourself you've severed and denied. About wholeness."

As she spoke, Phoenix was aware of a striking phenomenon—as if the room was gently reacting in sync with her words, the stars above vibrating with each truth that resonated within him.

"You fear that without rigid limitations, you would become unrecognizable to yourself," she continued. "That your desires, once acknowledged, would consume you entirely."

The accuracy of her perception startled him. "Wouldn't they?"

"Is that what you've observed in those who have honest desires? That they become slaves to it?" Her eyes held challenge now. "Or have you been taught to believe that credo by those who fear what they cannot control?" She brushed that wayward lock of hair from her forehead with a casual yet deliberate movement.

His minister friend's face appeared unbidden—the attempted suicide that had become one of the triggers for his current crisis. A man who had lived authentically, embracing his desires without shame, until the church's inquisition began.

"I had a friend," Phoenix began, surprised by the emotion thick in his throat as the face of his close friend appeared vividly in his mind—delicate eyes that had seen too much judgment, shoulders that had finally bent under the weight of others' expectations. "He lived ... openly, honestly. But, I fear he is too gentle for this world. He tried to kill himself six months ago."

Pauline's expression softened immediately. "*C'est terrible*," she said quietly, "do you believe it was his freedom, his gentleness, or the severe questioning that traumatized him?"

"I don't know," Phoenix acknowledged. "Maybe it was the world's response to his freedom."

Pauline looked serious. "Religion and culture can be cruel to those who refuse their constraints. Yet living a lie extracts its own type of punishment, does it not?"

His marriage surfaced in his mind, followed by his persona at church, the exhausting compartmentalization of public and private selves, and years of maintaining walls between parts of himself. "What do you want from me?" he asked finally.

"It's not about what I want," she replied. Her voice dropped to an intimate register that seemed to bypass his ears and speak directly to his skin. "It's about what you need. What you've needed for a long time and have forgotten how to recognize." She stood, cocktail in hand, her filmy dress silhouetting her full body. "Stand up, Phoenix," motioning with the glass.

He hesitated, uncertainty freezing him in place.

"You promised Mircea, did you not? To accept what is asked of you in this room?" Her tone was gentle but firm, and the hint of accent was more pronounced now.

Slowly, Phoenix rose from the chair, the leather releasing him with a soft sigh. Standing, he was taller than Pauline, yet somehow she maintained the position of authority between them.

"Remove your sweater," she said.

The request—or command—sent a jolt of alarm through him. "I don't—"

"You do," she interrupted. "You've wanted someone to ask this of you. To permit you to shed the layers you hide behind. C'est vrai, non?" She smiled, her eyes soft. "The body isn't meant to be hidden, mon cher. It's meant to be celebrated."

His hands moved to the seam of his sweater, then hesitated. The room's warmth seemed to intensify, and he became acutely aware of every layer between his skin and the air.

"The body is not shameful, Phoenix. It is the temple where pleasure and transcendence meet." She spoke the words not as clichés but as a simple truth. "Your religion claims to believe the same, yet teaches you to despise the vessel of your experience."

Her voice carried the weight of centuries of misunderstanding. Something in her tone—compassion devoid of judgment—caught him off guard. He remembered a passage from one of Lilith's art books, about Michelangelo viewing the human form as divine creation, worthy of celebration rather than concealment.

"Every culture has its myths about the body," Pauline continued, as if reading his thoughts. "But which serves truth, and which serves control?"

Phoenix felt the question penetrate his core. His fingers, still at his sweater's edge, twitched with indecision. Years of conditioning warred with this moment of potential liberation.

"I..." he began, then stopped. What was he terrified of? Not Pauline's judgment—her acceptance was evident. Not divine retribution—that fear seemed suddenly abstract. No, he realized, he feared his own response, his own awakening to possibility.

With trembling hands, he pulled the cashmere over his head, feeling goosebumps on his skin. He stood in his undershirt, acutely aware of how rarely he allowed himself to be exposed in any way.

"Now, the undergarment," Pauline said, her eyes holding his. There was approval in her gaze, an appreciation that contained encouragement and empathy.

His chest thumped as he removed the T-shirt. Standing bare-chested in the starlit room, Phoenix discerned a paradox of vulnerability and liberation. He had not stood like this in years, except in the medical context of examination rooms. To be seen—truly seen—by another was terrifying and exhilarating.

"*Magnifique,*" Pauline said, her gaze taking in his body without objectification, appreciating it as one might admire a sculpture or painting. "The body you've hidden and denied and taught yourself to be ashamed of. Look at it, Phoenix. See it as I do."

He glanced down at himself, seeing not the ordinary, aging body he usually perceived but an essential truth—the physical manifestation of his existence in the world. For a strange, suspended moment, he wondered at the simple fact of his embodiment.

"Now, let's continue," she said, moving closer to him, the heat of her body perceptible even without contact.

The command was unexpected, far beyond what he had anticipated; Phoenix took a step backward. "I can't do this," he said, his voice strangled. "Not with you—not with anyone—watching."

"*Pourquoi?* Why?" The question was penetrating but straightforward. "Who taught you that pleasure must be solitary and shameful? Who convinced you that your desire must be hidden?" She reached out, not quite touching him, her hand hovering near his chest.

He could feel her kinetic energy, and had no answer that didn't lead back to the religious doctrines he'd begun to question.

"In my novel," Pauline continued, "O discovers that being seen in her most vulnerable moments is liberating. That the gaze of another can be a mirror in which we finally recognize ourselves." She bent over, put down her cocktail, and opened the book, finding a passage without searching for it. "Listen: 'What would be the good of being free? In all the world, what is there to desire beyond this surrender?'"

The words reverberated in the circular room, penetrating directly to reality hidden within Phoenix. He remained standing, caught between the desire to flee and the more passionate desire to finally experience the freedom Pauline described.

"I'm not sure I can," he confessed, the admission costing him significantly.

Pauline's expression held no judgment, only compassion. "Your body knows, *mon trésor*. Trust it, as you've never allowed yourself to do." Her glance moved to his belt. "Continue."

Closing his eyes, Phoenix remembered his promise to Mircea, who had welcomed him to this room of wonders. Slowly, with fingers that still trembled, he unbuckled his belt and then the button of his jeans. The sound of the zipper seemed unnaturally loud in the quiet room.

"Open your eyes," Pauline said softly. "Hiding from the experience diminishes it. Be present for yourself."

He forced his eyes open, meeting her gaze. There was no mockery there, no prurient interest—only a sincere acceptance that melted the ice of his shame.

"It can be an act of worship, you know," she said, her voice taking on a reverent quality. "The celebration of pleasure. Many spiritual traditions understand this—Taoism, Kabbalah, tantra, and indigenous tribes worldwide. Only authoritarian religions have severed the connection between the sacred and the sensual." She again brushed a

hand through her dark hair, somehow casual yet haunt-
ingly sensual.

Phoenix let his jeans fall as she spoke, now standing
in only his boxer briefs. The last barrier. His arousal evident, his hand hovered at the waistband, courage failing
him.

"Tell me," Pauline said, changing approach, "what do
you fear will happen if you allow yourself this freedom?
That God will strike you down?" She touched her own
throat, a sign of vulnerability. "That you will be consumed
by lust and lose control of yourself? That you will discover
how much life you've wasted in denial?"

The last question struck home. A pressure built behind Phoenix's eyes, the threat of tears he rarely permitted himself. "All of it," he whispered.

"Yet here you are," she observed, her eyes softening.
"Already more honest than you've been with yourself in
years. Has lightning struck? Has your soul been corrupt-
ed? Or do you feel more comfortable in your skin than
you have since childhood?"

She smiled, a warm, encouraging expression that
seemed to reach out and steady him. She was right. Beneath the fear and embarrassment, Phoenix seemed
strangely alive, awakened to sensations and emotions long
buried.

"In *The Story of O*," Pauline continued, "there is a
moment when O realizes that her submission is not
weakness but strength. That in surrendering to her desires,
she becomes more fully herself." She turned a page.

"Here: 'She had never felt as light of heart, never as free, never as sure of herself.'"

He stood motionless, absorbing her words, feeling them reverberate within. A bead of sweat traced down his temple.

"Your religion has taught you that desire is your enemy," Pauline said. "I am here to suggest that it is your guide—the voice of your truest self calling you home." She reached out and lightly touched his arm, the contact brief but electric. "*Écoutez*. Listen to it."

With those words, the world shifted once again in Phoenix. A lifetime of prohibition and shame seemed to recede, not vanishing but losing its grip on him. With one move, he pulled down the last article of clothing, naked and exposed in the luminescence of Mircea's sanctum.

Pauline's gaze remained on his face; her expression was quiet pride as if he had passed some essential test. "Now," she said softly, "show yourself what pleasure without shame feels like."

As Phoenix hesitated, conflicting emotions battled within him. Flashes of ingrained shame quickly followed moments of liberation. His movements faltered, then resumed, his breathing uneven as competing narratives—the religious teachings of his past, the new perspective Pauline offered—fought for dominance in his consciousness.

"The conditioning runs deep," Pauline observed, noticing his struggle. "This is not overcome in a single moment but addressed one day at a time."

His hand moved to his hardening penis, the touch sending galvanic currents through his body. Unlike the furtive, hurried experiences of his past, this was honest and deliberate. His eyes remained open, Pauline watching him fully, seeing not the condemnation he had feared but a nurturing pride in his courage.

"Beautiful," she exclaimed as his movements grew more rhythmic. "This is what was stolen from you—not only physical pleasure but the revival of that pleasure into every fiber of your self. *Le plaisir est sacré*. Pleasure is sacred."

As Phoenix continued, gasping, a transformation overtook him. The shame he had expected to feel never materialized; in its place was a vast sense of rightness, of reclaiming a hidden truth that had always been his.

"In my novel," Pauline continued, her fingers tracing the edge of the page with deliberate sensuality, "O discovers that her body is not separate from her spirit—that her desires are not corrupt but essential to who she is."

She turned another page, the paper sighing softly beneath her touch. The sound drew his attention to her hands—elegant, expressive, moving with practiced grace.

Slowly sitting down, she crossed and recrossed her legs, revealing the skin above the top of her stockings. The subtle sound of silk against silk punctuated her words. "She highlights the contradiction that we sometimes experience the most intense pleasure when we relinquish control."

Phoenix felt himself approaching climax, the sensation building within him more powerful than anything he had ever experienced. His breathing became shallow, muscles tensing. Yet he hesitated, some last vestige of inhibition holding him back. His jaw clenched, fighting the very release his body sought.

"Let go," Pauline urged gently. "Physically, yes, and your mind also—release all the lies you've been told about your body, your desires, your right to pleasure." Her lips parted slightly, and the French phrase emerged like a caress: "*Laisse-toi aller.* Let it all go."

With those words, the final barrier dissolved. Surrendered utterly to the experience, his orgasm washed through him like a tidal wave. It encompassed his whole self—physical, mental, emotional, and yes, the spiritual— sheer bliss. As the powerful sensations subsided, his breathing gradually slowed, and his body relaxed in a way it hadn't in years. For a moment—one pure moment—he felt no shame at all.

"That…" Pauline said softly, "…is what transcendence feels like."

Then, like a reflex, Pastor Edwards' voice intruded: 'Sin feels good, Phoenix. That's why it's dangerous.' His muscles tensed, fingers reaching for his clothing. But something had changed. The shame rose, yes, but it didn't overwhelm him completely. It felt external somehow— programmed guilt, not innate truth.

"I don't know what to make of this," Phoenix conceded, feeling unsteady. Perhaps the peace wasn't permanent, but it had been real. "Part of me feels … relief. Another part is waiting for punishment." He realized this would be harder outside these walls, his hands still trembling.

She thoughtfully handed him linen napkins from the silver tray. "These are the first steps on a long journey," Pauline said gently. "Not total transformation, but the willingness to consider it. The seeds have been planted—they will grow in their own time."

He was quiet, understanding at a level beyond words. Slowly, without urgency, still shaking, he gathered his clothes.

"Your religion," Pauline continued, "speaks often of a 'born again' experience, that moment of spiritual transformation when one commits fully to your God. But they imagine it as a disembodied experience, a denial of sinful flesh. Yet, true rebirth happens here." She passionately hugged herself as if to symbolize his body, the room, and the sensual experience they had shared. "In the reclaiming of the wholeness that was always your birthright."

As Phoenix pulled his clothes back on, he looked different in them—as if his skin had somehow become more his own, his body more fully inhabited.

"You suspect there is no afterlife," Pauline said, again displaying her uncanny ability to read his thoughts. "That you have denied yourself pleasure in this life for a reward or punishment that may never come."

She picked up her cocktail again, taking a full mouthful of the amber-colored beverage. "*Mon Dieu!*" she again exclaimed after a deep swallow, her eyes closing in sensual pleasure.

"Speaking of *Dieu*," he said sarcastically, referring to her expletive, "Yes, I have begun to suspect there is no afterlife." He voiced the confession more easily now than an hour ago.

"What if heaven is not a place you go when you die," she suggested, "but a state you create while you live? A place of authenticity, sensuality, and the courage to embrace all aspects of your humanity." She set down her glass, the action elegant and thoughtful.

Deliberating this, he returned to his chair, sinking into it with a new awareness of his body's contact with the cool leather. "But I have a wife," returning to old justifications," Children. Responsibilities."

"What do they deserve from you?" Pauline asked, drawing closer. "The hollow shell you've become? Or a person fully alive, fully aware, capable of genuine connection?" There was a touch of sadness in her eyes. "*L'amour véritable*—True love demands truth, Phoenix. Always."

The question pierced Phoenix with its accuracy. How long had it been since Prudence had aroused him? How often had he performed the role of husband, father, friend, and executive while his true self remained locked away?

"*The Story of O* ends with a choice," Pauline said, placing the open book on the table. "O must decide between being with the man she loves or dying. But the true choice—the one that matters—has already been made. She has chosen to become fully herself, whatever the consequences. Your religion has taught you that certain desires are sinful. That they lead to destruction. Once again, has repressing them led to fulfillment?"

Her question contained no judgment, only genuine curiosity as she tilted her head, studying him with those perceptive eyes.

He realized she was right. Even now, analyzing these memories, his body had tensed, his breathing had become shallow, and his jaw had tightened. "Is there any way back?" he asked quietly. "After decades of this conditioning?"

"The body is remarkably resilient," Pauline said, her voice warm with conviction. "More forgiving than the mind, in many ways. It waits patiently for permission to remember its natural state." She wiggled in her chair, stretched out her shapely leg, and pointed the high heel in a ballet move. "Consider how a dancer who has not practiced for many years can still find the moves when the right music plays. The body remembers."

"What's the first step?" Phoenix asked, surprising himself with his willingness to consider change.

"Awareness," Pauline replied. "Notice how your body feels in various moments—when you're alone, with others, when you speak of certain topics. Notice where your breath catches, where you feel arousal, where you feel expansion or contraction." Her expression was gentle but firm. "Don't judge these responses; recognize them. This awareness itself begins to loosen the conditioning."

Slowly, he nodded. It was a simple suggestion, yet profoundly challenging—to pay attention to the very sensations he'd been taught to ignore or suppress. "I could try that," he said cautiously.

"*C'est un début*—it's a beginning," Pauline said encouragingly. "The journey back to embodiment happens one response at a time. Not a sudden revolution, but a gradual remembering of what was always yours."

Again, sensing change within, he felt the first minor loosening of a knot tied long ago. It wasn't freedom, not yet, but the recognition that freedom might be possible. He understood now why this had to be the second encounter, following his awakening to curiosity with Beatrix. Without that first opening of his mind to questions, he might not have been ready for this reclaiming of his body, of his right to pleasure and desire.

"Will I remember this?" he asked, a new fear arising, "Or will it fade like a dream when I leave this room?"

Pauline's expression illuminated her face with genuine compassion. "That depends on you, *mon cher*. Whether you carry this experience onward or return to the comfortable numbness of before." She inclined toward him, her eyes holding his with gentle fervor. "Having awakened this beautiful part of yourself, can you bear to let it die again?

Knowing the answer before consciously forming it, he answered, "No." Whatever this strange experience was—hallucination, dream, mystical visitation—he could not return to the half-life he had been living. The door that had opened could not be closed again.

Pauline's form seemed to shimmer in the afterglow, becoming less substantial. "My time with you draws to a close," she said, her voice remaining clear despite her increasingly translucent appearance. "Remember this: your

RANDY ELROD

body is not the enemy. In repressing it, you have denied yourself access to the wholeness of your self."

She held up his burgundy chronicle so that he could see the writing:

> "Remember this: your body is not the enemy. In repressing it, you have denied yourself access to the wholeness of your self."

The desire to ask more questions made him want to prolong this atypical conversation. Still, he could feel a heaviness descending over him—not unpleasant, but insistent, like the approach of sleep after intense exertion.

"*Merci*," he said as Pauline's form grew fainter, "Thank you so much."

Her face was the last part to fade. "Remember," her distant voice came to him, "pleasure is your birthright. Claim it without shame. It pleases me, this courage of yours. *Au revoir, mon* brave Phoenix."

oooo

She was gone, leaving him alone in the circular room. *The Story of O* was back on his side table and closed as if no one had ever opened it. Yet Phoenix could feel the evidence of his experience in the lingering afterglow of pleasure, relaxed muscles, and the soothing sense of peace that reached beyond his intellect, touching something primordial within. As he considered this new freedom from sexual constraints, his thoughts inexplicably turned to Dion.

Unable to sort it all out, he leaned back in the chair, allowing his eyes to close. The rays from above seemed to penetrate his eyelids, bathing him in gentle radiance. For the first time in longer than he could remember, Phoenix felt at home in his skin, relishing the beauty of his body, no longer fighting to repress it.

As he savored this feeling of release, hovering at the edge of sleep, doubt began to settle back upon him. What had seemed so clear in Pauline's presence now felt ephemeral.

'This can't be real,' he thought, rationality reasserting itself. 'Some strange effect of the libations? Who was he to discard decades of teaching based on these encounters?'

Yet his body remembered what his mind questioned. The tension had not fully returned to his shoulders. His mind remained more open, curious, questioning—transformed by Beatrix's guidance. And now his body had begun its awakening under Pauline's care.

He was suspended between worlds now—the one he'd always known and something else just beginning to take shape. Not completely transformed, but no longer unchanged either.

# Interlude - Dion

The conversations with Pauline and Beatrix swirled through his mind like leaves caught in an autumn eddy, fragments of wisdom settling in unexpected places. His body seemed impossibly lightweight as if decades had been temporarily lifted from his shoulders.

A whisper of familiarity and a change in the room's scent brought him back. He opened his eyes to find the ceiling above had subtly altered its configuration, now forming constellations he had never seen but somehow recognized. The Purging Room remained, its circular perfection unchanged, but the air now carried a bouquet of juniper and citrus and a more primal aroma—earth after rain, forest floor at dawn.

"You're here," came a melodious voice. "Welcome back."

Dion stood beside the small bar, arranging bottles with the deliberate grace of a musician selecting instruments. Gone was the formal attire from earlier; now, he wore a simple white shirt, open at the throat, its sleeves rolled to reveal forearms corded with subtle strength. His dark curls caught the starlight, creating a halo-like effect. "How long was I ...." Phoenix began, uncertain how to describe what had happened.

"Time moves differently here," Dion replied with a smile that transformed his face from beautiful to transcendent. "You've traversed two thresholds already, which is more than most accomplish in a single visit."

"Would you care for an aperitif?" Dion asked, his hands moving among the bottles with knowing familiarity. "After such journeys, a refreshing libation to ground you might be welcome."

Phoenix stood up and stretched, aware of an intense thirst. "Yes, thank you."

Dion's movements as he mixed drinks were mesmerizing—economical yet smooth, practiced yet improvisational. He selected a heavy crystal decanter containing an bright green spirit and added several drops from tiny bottles of different colors, each unstoppered and restoppered with choreographed finesse.

"What are you making?" Phoenix asked, curiosity awakened by Beatrix Potter's gentle guidance.

Dion's eyes flicked up, with a coy wink. "A mixture appropriate for this moment in your journey. Another invention of mine."As he spoke, he poured the concoction into a glass that seemed to have been carved from a single piece of ice but showed no signs of melting. It resembled a liquid emerald in the glass, with rich amber highlights when it catches the light.

Dion crossed the room and handed over the glass, his fingers brushing Phoenix's in a contact that seemed accidental yet deliberate enough to send a fluttering sensation up his arm that momentarily confused him. The feeling differed from what he'd experienced with Pauline, but was equally appealing.

"You've begun to change already," Dion observed, settling gracefully onto a low stool that Phoenix hadn't noticed before. The position placed Dion below his eye level, creating an unexpected intimacy. "I can see it in how you hold yourself, how your eyes take in the room."

As Phoenix sipped the mysterious potion, its flavor unfolded on his palate like a tale told in multiple languages simultaneously—sweet herbaceous notes, followed by citrus and juniper botanicals and finishing with a rich velvety mouthfeel. It produced an exhilaration that spread from his core to his extremities. "What am I supposed to be experiencing here?" he asked, surprised by his candor.

Dion laughed, the sound reminiscent of festivities and merrymaking. "There she is—Beatrix's influence already at work. A question instead of an assumption." He moved closer toward Phoenix, hands clasping his chin and elbows resting on his knees. "There is no 'supposed to,' Phoenix. That's the first lesson of this room. There is only what you discover, release, and become."

Taking another sip, Phoenix allowed the complex flavors to linger on his tongue. The liquor seemed to dissolve barriers—not his perception, which remained clear—but restrictive thoughts and feelings he had maintained rigidly for decades.

"What have you discovered so far?" Dion queried.

"Pauline showed me..." he began, then paused, still struggling to articulate what had transpired.

"She showed you to be proud of your body," Dion supplied, his expression open and affirming. "That pleasure is not separate from the body but an expression of it."

Relieved at not having to explain, Phoenix breathed deeply and became the questioner, "Beatrix?"

"Reminded you that questions cannot threaten true belief but can deepen it," Dion continued. "That curiosity is not childish but one of the most profoundly adult qualities we can cultivate."

"You understand," Phoenix observed.

"I know the stages of transformation," Dion replied with a slight shrug that contained modesty and ancient wisdom. "I've witnessed them countless times in this room, though each unfolding is unique to the seeker."

"What's your role in all this?" Phoenix asked, the question emerging from a newly awakened curiosity.

Dion mulled this, his head tilting.

"I am the space between their words and your experience," he said. "The bridge between concept and embodiment." His smile returned, enlivening his features. "Pauline and Beatrix can guide you to freedom of body and mind. I live it every day."

As if to demonstrate, Dion rose in a single fluid movement. He returned to the bar, his body expressing a harmony that Phoenix had rarely witnessed—utterly comfortable in his skin. Every step seemed spontaneous and inevitable, personifying with movement the principles the two women had conveyed through words.

With delicate expertise, Dion added a single drop of dark bitters to his glass, which appeared to contain a clear spirit. The drop shimmered with iridescence the moment it entered it.

"The next thresholds you'll cross," Dion said, motioning toward the books remaining to be opened, "will ask you to cultivate what you've begun to discover."

Glancing at the books, Phoenix sensed both anticipation and trepidation. The first two encounters had already shaken foundations he believed immovable.

"Are you afraid?" Dion asked, his perception acute.

"Yes," Phoenix conceded, finding straightforwardness easier now than earlier.

"Good," Dion smiled. "Remember, fear is the body's recognition that a significant moment approaches. It doesn't mean stop—it means pay attention." He moved closer again, his energy radiating a sensuality that seemed to penetrate Phoenix's cells.

Phoenix finished, the final sip releasing new layers of flavor he hadn't noticed initially, as if the beverage had transformed as he consumed it. "What if I can't go back?" he asked, voicing the concern that had been growing since his encounter with Pauline. "To my life, my work, my ... marriage." The last word caught in his throat.

Dion took the empty glass from Phoenix's hand, and the touch of his fingers again created that momentary connection that felt like communion between them. "The better question may be: what if you can return as someone new? Someone who carries these experiences within him?"

The question reframed Phoenix's fears in a way that opened possibilities, not closed them. He hadn't weighed that option—bringing new awareness into the contexts he had always known.

"The most immeasurable transformations," Dion said, voice gentle now, "don't always require an external revolution. Sometimes, they're internal evolutions that gradually reshape our relationship to every aspect of our lives."

Phoenix sensed an open-minded confidence that whatever awaited him, he could meet it with newfound resources.

"You should relax before continuing," Dion suggested, returning to the bar with Phoenix's glass. "The next two thresholds require attention."

Eyes fluttering, Phoenix knew that a pleasant fatigue was working through his system.

"Dion," he said as the young man reached the bar, "once again, I can't say thank you enough." He turned, and momentarily, Phoenix saw ancient discernment in his eyes that belied his youthful appearance—wisdom born of countless cycles of reconstruction and rebirth.

"Remember," Dion whispered, "some journeys divide us from what we've known, while others connect us to what we've forgotten. Your true self awaits in the spaces between." With those words, he seemed to blend into the room's ambient luster, not vanishing but becoming less distinct, as if Phoenix's perception of him was softening around the edges.

oooo

Rather than drifting toward sleep, Phoenix felt suddenly, vibrantly alert. The room around him seemed to respond to this wakefulness, the circular walls beginning to shift. At first, he thought it might be an optical illusion—a trick of the starlight above—but then the movement became unmistakable. The walls were breathing.

Expanding and contracting with deliberate rhythm, the chamber pulsed like some great living organism. The bookshelves undulated in waves, their countless volumes rising and falling in perfect harmony as if riding an invisible tide. With each inhalation, the room expanded, creating space that logic insisted couldn't exist; with each exhalation, it drew inward, bringing distant objects closer without ever feeling confining.

Phoenix placed his hand on the arm of his chair to steady himself. Beneath his fingers, the leather developed a hypnotic rhythm, matching the room's respiration. He felt a moment of dizzying wonder—was he inside some enormous living thing? Or had the room itself developed consciousness?

The tempo of the breathing walls began to affect his physiology. His nervous system adjusted, synchronizing with the room's pulsations. Each breath he took aligned perfectly with the chamber's respiration, creating an uncanny connection between his body and surroundings. The boundary between observer and observed was dissolving.

As the walls continued their rhythmic movement, the room's texture transformed. The warm, sensual glow that had illuminated his conversation with Pauline changed, becoming cooler and more concrete. Colors deepened and clarified, edges sharpened, and shadows receded. It was as if the entire space was focusing itself, moving from the dreamlike realm of sensuality to the crystalline domain of emotion.

The bookshelves rippled like waves against a shore, rearranging their contents. Volumes of illustrated children's classics and erotica slid back into the shelves, while psychology texts and philosophy studies emerged.

The starlight above coalesced into new patterns—more ordered and deliberate, as if the cosmos were mathematically mapped. Constellations transformed from sensual renderings to precise coordinate systems, stars connecting with gleaming lines that formed complex geometric figures.

The walls took a particularly huge breath, expanding to their fullest extent and contracting deliberately. The midnight blue chair opposite him, empty since Pauline's departure, mutated as they did. The color intensified, the shape became more structured, and the cushions were firmed as if preparing for a different occupant.

His cocktail had also transformed—no longer the amber-colored libation he'd enjoyed with Pauline but a lime-green drink rimmed with salt and spice.

As he registered these changes, the chair opposite was suddenly occupied by a man in his sixties, wire-framed glasses catching the transformed light, his body radiating the contained energy of someone whose mind worked at perpetual high speed.

"Fascinating!" the man exclaimed without introduction. He held Phoenix's mystical book, which he placed on the side table beside his blue chair. Immediately, he raised his hands to frame Phoenix's face from a distance, as if capturing it for analysis.

# CHAPTER SEVEN

## Emotional Amputation

The gentleman wore a tweed jacket with leather elbow patches over a blue oxford shirt, giving him the appearance of a professor from a more dignified era. Yet there was nothing staid or formal about his posture—he sat with a vibrant energy barely contained, as if he might leap from the chair at any moment. One leg crossed over the other, bouncing, his fingers tapping on the arm of the chair, and his face displayed rapidly shifting expressions that Phoenix could barely track.

"Your affect display suggests at least three simultaneous emotional states—interest-excitement predominant, but with undertones of surprise-startle and mild shame-humiliation. The tripolarity is particularly evident in the ocular musculature." He pulled a small notebook from his pocket and jotted words with quick, energetic movements.

Squinting, Phoenix was caught off guard by this clinical yet collegial assessment. "I'm sorry, what?"

"Your face," the man clarified, his features arranging themselves into a grin that radiated genuine pleasure. "It's telling at least three emotional stories at once. Most people show only one or two at a time—you're wonderfully expressive, though I suspect you've spent years trying to suppress that quality." He scribbled another note, then looked up abruptly. "Oh. Forgive me. Habit—I get so caught up in the observation that I forget simple courtesies."

"You're Silvan Tomkins," Phoenix said, recognition dawning.

"In the flesh—or some approximation thereof. Good to see you, Phoenix." Tomkins shrugged as if his existence were the least interesting topic.

Picking up the bound manuscript and turning it over in his hands, Phoenix examined its scholarly cover. It was the top folder of what appeared to be a multi-volume set labeled *Affect Theory* in precise handwriting, with 'Tomkins' scrawled in the corner. Opening it revealed typewritten pages dense with handwritten corrections in blue and black ink. Cigarette burns punctuated several margins, and coffee rings stained some corners.

Hand-drawn diagrams illustrated emotional states, with arrows connecting concepts in an intricate web. The pages carried the scent of old paper, tobacco, and intellectual fervor—the raw, unfiltered workings of a brilliant mind captured before official publication smoothed its edges.

He'd heard of Tomkins' work in a psychology elective during college—the groundbreaking theory that proposed all human emotions stemmed from nine innate biological affects hardwired into our neurology from birth.

Tomkin's hands moved as though conventional body language couldn't contain his enthusiasm. "Mircea somehow managed to secure my original draft. Seeing it brings back memories. You are holding my life's work in your hands."

"Now, let's talk about you. You've had a revelatory journey through body and mind. Beatrix and Pauline have done their work well." He stretched even further forward, his eyes alight with enthusiasm. "Now, we bridge those realms—the emotional landscape that connects mental understanding with physical response. Isn't that exciting?"

The stars above again seemed to pulse in time with his words, casting intriguing patterns across the circular room.

Tomkins rapidly stood, the shift so abrupt that Phoenix instinctively straightened in his chair. The older man paced in a small circle, his energy reminiscent of a conductor about to direct an orchestra."Before I was a psychologist," Tomkins said, pivoting to face Phoenix, "I taught drama. Did you know that? Most don't."

His body moved expressively as he spoke, punctuating his words with gestures that seemed to shape the concepts he described physically. "That background wasn't incidental to my later work—it was foundational. To un-

derstand emotion, you must first recognize its performance." He demonstrated this by quickly transforming
his face into an expression of exaggerated wonder, then
quickly shifting to contemplation and then to amusement—the transitions so seamless they seemed almost
like watching a film.

Tomkins' animated presence transfixed Phoenix. The
psychologist embodied a paradoxical quality that Phoenix
had rarely witnessed—a complete unselfconsciousness
that coexisted with remarkable self-awareness as if he had
mastered the art of living fully present while maintaining
complete insight into his nature.

"I studied emotional theories in college," Phoenix
ventured, drawing on his limited knowledge of psychology. "Freud's drives, cognitive approaches… "

Tomkins made a sound somewhere between a laugh
and a snort. "Drives. As if hunger and sex explain the full
spectrum of human emotional experience." He motioned
as if physically brushing away those inadequate theories.

"Imagine describing a symphony as merely the product of strings vibrating or wind moving through tubes.
Technically correct but utterly missing the point." He
rapped his temple emphatically. "It's like claiming you
understand Shakespeare because you know the alphabet.
Woefully inadequate."

"This all sounds very theoretical," Phoenix said after
Tomkins' initial explanation of affects. "But real life isn't
so neat. Emotions are messy, unpredictable."

"The weather is also complex," Tomkins countered,
light catching his glasses as he tilted his head. "Yet under-

standing the basic principles of meteorology helps us navigate storms. We don't need to predict every raindrop to recognize a hurricane is forming."

"Affects aren't just theoretical concepts," Tomkins said, abandoning his professorial posture to lean in with conspiratorial intimacy. "They saved me from bankruptcy during the Depression."

Phoenix's expression shifted to surprise. "How so?"

"Horse racing," Tomkins replied with a mischievous glint. "While other men bet on names or numbers, I watched the horses—their affect displays before races tell everything about their condition." He mimicked studying something intently. "The slight ear movements, the dilation of nostrils, the muscle tension along the neck—all signals of interest-excitement versus distress-anguish."

"You read horses the way you read people?" Phoenix asked.

Tomkins laughed, a warm sound that transformed his scholarly demeanor. "Made enough to fund my research for three years." His expression sobered. "Though I learned my limits at the poker table. My wife—a brilliant woman who is better at masking her emotions than anyone I've met—could clean me out every payday until I finally admitted some mysteries remain even to affect theorists."

He rubbed the worn leather patches on his elbows thoughtfully. "That's how I learned affects aren't just to be studied but experienced. There's a difference between knowing anger's facial signatures and feeling the heat of it in your chest when someone you love is threatened."

Phoenix noticed how Tomkins' theoretical confidence gave way to genuine emotion as he spoke of his wife—a glimpse of the man behind the academic framework.

"Once, at a post office," Tomkins continued, "I pointed to a man on the FBI Most Wanted posters—told the clerk something was wrong with the image. Two weeks later, they discovered it was the wrong man entirely." He shrugged. "The misalignment between the displayed and genuine emotion was obvious, though at that time I couldn't explain why to others. The body knows, Phoenix. It always knows."

Still skeptical, Phoenix asked, "So I just need to ... feel my feelings? That seems overly simplified."

"Not merely feel them," Tomkins clarified, "but recognize what they're communicating. Like learning a new language." He returned to his chair but perched on its edge, unwilling to surrender his animated energy to the comfort of settling back. "Let me ask you this, Phoenix—what are you feeling right now? Not thinking, feeling."

His eyes fixed on Phoenix's face with fascination. The straightforwardness of the question caught Phoenix off guard. He'd spent countless years in environments where emotions were either suppressed (business) or channeled into approved expressions (church), and identifying his genuine feelings had indeed become a foreign exercise.

"I'm interested," he said finally. "Curious about what you're going to say. A little confused. Somewhat apprehensive." As he spoke, Phoenix again spied the cocktails. They were in glass coupes with slender stems. He grabbed the chance and tasted the drink, surprised that it was rum-based, not tequila.

"Good, good." Tomkins nodded vigorously, jotting more in his notebook. "Now watch." He immediately transformed his face into an exaggerated expression of interest—eyebrows raised, eyes widened, mouth narrowly open. He swapped to confusion with theatrical precision—brows furrowed, head tilted, lips pursed. Finally, apprehension—eyes darting, shoulders hunched, mouth tense.

"What you described aren't three different emotions," Tomkins explained, his face returning to its animated baseline. "They're variations and combinations of what I call affects. Interest-excitement, surprise-startle, and fear-terror—three of the nine basic emotions that form the foundation of all human experience."

"These aren't learned, Phoenix. They're biological. Built into the human operating system from birth. Good heavens. Even newborns display them!" His eyes widened at the wonder of it.

Leaning forward, Phoenix was immediately curious. "Only nine?"

"Only nine," Tomkins confirmed with evident delight at Phoenix's interest, slapping his knee for emphasis. "Isn't that marvelous? Everything else—every complex emotional state you've ever experienced—combines these basic affects, coupled with your memory and cognition." He jumped up again, too energized to remain seated.

"That's the first revelation—emotions aren't infinite and unknowable. They're finite and identifiable. Like primary colors mixing to create endless variations." He made a sweeping indication as if painting the air with a broad brush.

"My religion teaches that emotions are dangerous, particularly the negative ones. That they lead us astray, into sin," Phoenix responded.

Tomkins stopped his pacing and fixed Phoenix with a penetrating look. "There are no negative emotions," he said firmly, touching his finger to his thumb like a professor making a crucial point. "There are only negative responses to emotions. Each affect serves a vital function in the human experience. That's like calling rain negative because sometimes it causes floods. Absurd."

He moved again, but more deliberately now, using his body to illustrate his points. "Anger tells you when lines have been crossed. Fear alerts you to potential threats. Shame binds you to social norms that facilitate communal living."

His hands carved shapes in the air as he spoke. "Even disgust serves a purpose—it helped our ancestors avoid poisonous or rotten food. Would you call that negative? I certainly wouldn't."

Phoenix thought about this. "Some emotions feel negative. Unhealthy."

"Yes, they do," Tomkins agreed enthusiastically. "Nature designed them that way. Anxiety feels bad because it needs to get your attention. Same with fear, anguish, and disgust."

He paused, pointing a finger at Phoenix. "But here's the crucial distinction—feeling bad isn't the same as being bad. That's the emotional amputation your religion has performed—equating unpleasant with immoral." He drew his finger across his throat in a cutting motion. "Slash! Off with everything that doesn't feel pleasant. Quite barbaric when you think about it."

The phrase "emotional amputation" struck Phoenix like a physical blow. His hand rose involuntarily to his chest, as if protecting a wound.

Tomkins noticed the reaction immediately, his eyes narrowing with interest. "Aha! That phrase resonated, didn't it? I can see the distress-anguish in your facial muscles, particularly around the eyes." He returned to his chair, leaning toward Phoenix with newfound gentleness.

"Tell me about this amputation. What parts of your emotional self have you cut away to fit into the containers others built for you?" His voice had softened, but his gaze remained keenly observant.

The question penetrated deeply, and Phoenix was momentarily speechless. Images flashed through his mind: swallowing anger during church meetings when doctrine contradicted compassion, suppressing excitement about ideas that fell outside approved thinking, and hiding his shame from everyone, even himself, until it became a constant, unacknowledged companion.

"Everything," he affirmed, the confession again costing him considerably. "Anything that didn't fit the pattern of the successful businessman, the devoted husband, the committed church elder."

"Tell me about a time when you learned emotions were dangerous," Tomkins said, drawing closer eagerly.

oooo

Phoenix closed his eyes; the childhood memory was immediate and graphic. He was seven at his grandfather's funeral. The tightness in his throat, the hot tears he couldn't stop. His father's grip on his shoulder was painfully tight. "That's enough. Men don't cry like that." The drive home was silent, and his father's disappointment was a physical presence in the car. "Pull yourself together. Your mother needs you to be strong."

oooo

He met Silvan's waiting gaze. "I was seven," Phoenix said. "My grandfather's funeral. I learned that grief was a luxury men couldn't afford."

"And anger?" Tomkins prompted, watching Phoenix's face intently. "When did you learn to swallow that?"

oooo

A flash of memory: twelve years old, furious about getting benched during the championship game despite being the team's best player. He'd slammed the door when they got home. His father's voice, deadly quiet: "God is watching your tantrum. Is this who you want to be? A man ruled by his emotions rather than ruling them?" The shame that had followed, the suppression of the anger until it settled as a hard knot in his stomach, where it had lived ever since.

oooo

The memory's weight settled in his chest as he described it to Silvan. "Twelve," Phoenix said. "I learned that anger was a spiritual failure. That emotion needed to be conquered, not expressed."

"Fascinating," Tomkins exclaimed, but his tone had softened from academic interest to compassionate understanding. "You know, I had a similar experience as a boy. My father was a Methodist minister—quite stern, quite controlled. When my dog died, I was inconsolable. He told me my grief was an affront to God, who had more important concerns than a child's pet."

Tomkins' eyes grew distant for a moment. "I went behind the woodshed and howled where no one could hear me. Even at ten, I recognized something profoundly wrong in being told my feelings were inappropriate. That experience shaped my entire career, though I didn't realize it until decades later."

"You and I were taught to perform stoicism rather than experience authentic emotion. No wonder your affect display shows such complexity—parts of you have been fighting for expression for decades." Tomkins' eyes focused on his face, showing neither surprise nor judgment.

"The emotional scripts we learn early become the directors of our lives unless we consciously rewrite them.

Like the script that taught you at age seven that 'men don't cry,' which has directed how you've handled grief for forty years. This happens not just at funerals but in business failures, disappointments, and moments of beauty that moved you to tears you couldn't shed."

He tapped the book in Phoenix's lap, his touch gentle but emphatic. "That's the second revelation of affect theory—emotions are both biological and biographical. The basic affects are hardwired, but how we interpret and express them is learned." He ran a hand through his hair, leaving it disheveled.

The scholarly density of *Affect Theory* suddenly a bit less intimidating, Phoenix asked, "Did you say scripts?"

"Yes!" Tomkins exclaimed, nearly bouncing in his seat with renewed animation. "Think of these scripts as emotional programs written based on early experiences."

He rose suddenly, unable to contain his enthusiasm. With theatrical precision, he adopted the stern posture of an authority figure, finger wagging in admonishment.

"When a child is punished for showing anger, they internalize the message: 'Anger is dangerous—suppress it.'" Then, shifting his bearing to mimic a different character, he deepened his voice. "When a boy hears that 'real men don't cry,' he learns 'Distress must be hidden.'"

Phoenix nodded slowly, recognizing himself in both scenarios. "My father used those exact words," he said quietly.

Tomkins returned to his seat, facing him directly. His fingers mimed typing on an invisible keyboard. "These scripts become automatic, running below consciousness, like software perpetually operating in the background."

"And I've been running this ... software ... without knowing it," Phoenix said, the realization registering physically as a tightness in his chest.

"Exactly! And not just one program." Tomkins tapped his fingers against his temple, "Your church wrote scripts about shame and fear. Your business culture wrote scripts about acceptable expressions of enthusiasm or disappointment."

A memory surfaced—Phoenix reprimanding an employee for showing too much disappointment over a lost client. Had he been enforcing the same emotional constraints he resented?

"Even your marriage has its emotional screenplay," Tomkins continued, watching the recognition dawn on Phoenix's face. "With some feelings given starring roles and others left on the cutting room floor." He pantomimed, chopping with his hand, sending imaginary film strips flying. "Quite a heavy-handed editor you've become with your emotional life!"

Tomkins paused, a wry smile forming. "You know, after I published my first paper on affects, a colleague accused me of 'intellectualizing emotions to avoid feeling them.' I was furious—couldn't sleep for days." He chuckled, shaking his head. "He was completely right, of course. I'd become so fascinated with the mechanics of emotion that I'd neglected my own. Ironic, isn't it? The emotion expert emotionally stunted."

He mimed taking off glasses and cleaning them, though he continued wearing them. "My wife pointed it out most clearly. After giving a three-hour lecture on the importance of expressing anger appropriately, I came home to find she'd rearranged my study. Instead of telling her I was upset, I gave her a comprehensive analysis of the affect of anger, complete with citations to my research."

He laughed genuinely. "She threw a book at me—ironically, my own work—and said 'Stop telling me about anger and just be angry, you impossible man.'"

Phoenix smiled empathically at this glimpse of Tomkins' struggles with the very concepts he studied.

"In my business, leadership seminars teach us to 'manage' emotions rather than experience them. I attended an executive coaching session where we practiced 'controlled displays of passion' to motivate teams while maintaining what they called 'leadership distance.'"

"Fascinating," Tomkins exclaimed. "Emotional performance rather than emotional authenticity."

"Last year, I had to lay off thirty-two employees after a merger," Phoenix continued, his voice growing quieter. "The HR consultant advised me to show 'appropriate concern without excessive empathy' because 'emotional contagion could disrupt the transition process.'"

"And how did that feel?" Tomkins asked, adjusting his body slightly.

"Horrible," Phoenix admitted. "I was genuinely devastated for these people. Some had been with me for years. But I maintained the script—firm handshake, eye contact, brief acknowledgment of their service, then redirect to the severance package details."

"What happened to your authentic emotional response?"

"I went to the parking garage after the last meeting and sat in my car for an hour," Phoenix said. "Couldn't drive. Couldn't call anyone. Just sat there feeling ... nothing." He paused. "No, that's not true. Feeling everything but allowing myself to express nothing."

"The corporate world," Tomkins observed, "has created an aberrant emotional amputation—celebrating certain emotions like enthusiasm for profit while pathologizing authentic responses to human suffering."

"We even have metrics for it now," Phoenix added with a bitter laugh. "Our company tracks 'emotional intelligence scores' on performance reviews. One of the criteria is 'maintains appropriate emotional boundaries.'"

"Appropriate according to whom?" Tomkins asked, eyes bright with interest.

"Exactly," Phoenix replied. "I've never thought to question that before."

The accuracy of Silvan's assessments were unsettling. Phoenix had never thought about his emotional life in these terms, yet the framework Tomkins offered made sense of patterns he'd never been able to articulate. "How do you rewrite these scripts?" he asked, a new urgency in his voice.

"First, you recognize them," Tomkins replied, settling into a more professorial mode, though his body still seemed charged with energy. "Notice when an emotion arises and what narrative you immediately tell yourself about it. 'I shouldn't feel this way. This is inappropriate. This is sinful.'"

He mimicked these repressive responses with theatrical distaste, his face contorting into exaggerated expressions of self-judgment. "Ask yourself: Who taught me this interpretation? Is it serving me now? What would happen if I allowed this emotion its natural expression?" He spread his arms wide. "What would happen if you just let yourself feel angry when you're angry? Excited when you're excited? Afraid when you're afraid?"

Beatrix's encouragement to honor curiosity rather than suppress it resounded within Phoenix, alongside. Pauline's guidance toward experiencing pleasure without shame. Each encounter had peeled away another layer of his conditioning. "If emotions are biological, why must they be managed?" he asked. "Why not feel everything fully?"

Tomkins laughed with appreciation, clapping his hands once. "An excellent question. Egads! What a mind you have when you let it work."

Surging forward again, the psychologist continued, "We're social creatures living in complex environments. Pure emotional expression without modulation would make civilization untenable." With theatrical flair, Tomkins pantomimed a person in a rage, destroying everything around them.

As he did, lightning flashed across the starlit sky.

"Imagine if I expressed every flash of anger by throwing furniture. We'd be having this conversation amid splinters."

"There's a world of difference between healthy management and unhealthy denial," he explained with another slight lunge. "One acknowledges the emotion while choosing its expression; the other refuses to recognize the feeling exists." His hands formed a barrier before him, then slowly lowered. "The first is wisdom; the second is warfare against your nature."

Rising to his feet, Tomkins moved to the center of the circular room where the brilliance seemed to concentrate. "Let me demonstrate. Stand up, Phoenix." He beckoned with both hands, his energy hard to resist.

Surprised by the request, Phoenix complied, rising from his chair to join Tomkins in the room's center.

"Now, I want you to express anger physically," Tomkins instructed. "Don't think about it—embody it. Show me what it looks like when Phoenix Adams is furious."

Hesitating, feeling self-conscious, Phoenix stumbled, "I'm not sure how to—"

"Exactly," Tomkins interrupted, pointing triumphantly. "You've thoroughly dissociated from important emotional expressions and can't even simulate them on command. The pathway has been severed."

He moderated his tone, becoming gentler. "Try this instead. Think of a time when someone violated an important boundary—took an object that mattered to you, disrespected a valuable possession. Let your body remember."

Phoenix thought immediately of his father dismissing his early writing ambitions, of church elders shutting down his theological questions, of Prudence's cold rejection of his physical needs.

Without realizing it, his hands had clenched into fists, his jaw had tightened, and his posture had become more erect.

"There it is," Tomkins said softly, circling Phoenix slowly, observing with keen interest, "Hints of anger-rage. Not destructive in itself—it's telling you important information about your limits, your values, and your needs." His voice took on a respectful quality. "What is this anger saying to you right now?"

Closing his eyes, Phoenix fully experienced the response coursing through his body. "That I've been diminished. That parts of me have been treated as dispensable or dangerous when they're essential."

"Yes," Tomkins agreed, gentler now. "Anger is often a response to injustice—including injustice done to yourself—by yourself or others." He placed his fingers lightly on Phoenix's shoulders. "Now, notice how this emotion feels in your body. The tightness in your muscles, the heat in your face, the energy gathering in your core. This is information, Phoenix. Vital information your system is trying to communicate."

As he opened his eyes, Phoenix was surprised to find them somewhat damp. His anger had shifted, becoming more complex—grief mingled with determination.

"Now, interest-excitement," Tomkins continued, removing his hands and stepping back. "Think of an activity that genuinely fascinates you, that makes you lean forward, that you could explore for hours without tiring—that makes time disappear."

Phoenix thought of his early love of writing, creating worlds and characters, and the philosophical ideas that had captivated him in college before he'd learned to avoid them. Surprisingly, Dion came to mind—the young man's integrated grace and spirit.

Without conscious direction, his posture changed. His eyes widened, his breathing quickened, and a slight smile formed at the corners of his mouth.

"Beautiful!" Tomkins observed, circling Phoenix again. "Your entire system is saying, 'Yes, more of this, please.' Interest-excitement is the affect of exploration, of growth, of learning. It keeps us engaged with life instead of merely enduring it."

He stretched his arms towards Phoenix's transformed posture. "This is what your system hungers for—the freedom to follow what genuinely interests you, not what others have deemed appropriate or useful. Look at you. Seemingly years younger just from feeling genuine interest!"

They continued through several more emotions before returning to their chairs, Phoenix feeling physically tired but mentally more alert than he had in years.

"The third revelation of affect theory," Tomkins said, settling back into his seat but still radiating energy, "is that emotions are contagious. We catch them from others, and others catch them from us. Your emotional state affects everyone around you, whether you intend it or not."

He made a rippling motion with his hands. "Like dropping a stone in a pond—the ripples move outward, touching everything."

"I discovered this by accident in my own family," Tomkins confessed, his animated features softening. "My son was going through a difficult period—fighting at school, grades dropping. I approached it analytically, with charts and behavior modification plans." He grimaced at the memory.

"One evening, I found him crying in his room. Instead of analyzing it, for once I just sat with him, let myself feel his sadness. When I started to tear up too, he looked at me with such surprise. 'Dad, you never cry,' he said. That moment changed our relationship completely. My willingness to share his emotion rather than manage it opened something between us that all my theories couldn't touch."

oooo

Phoenix's marriage again came to mind, and the chilly emotional climate he and Prudence had created together for decades. His daughters, gleaning emotional repression by example.

And his affair with Lilith, with moments of genuine emotional connection like gulps of air after too long underwater.

oooo

"When my daughter Faith was seven," Phoenix said, surprised by the memory's clarity, "she painted this wild, colorful bird that didn't exist in nature. When I asked what kind of bird it was, she said, 'It's the one that lives in my heart, Daddy.' I praised her creativity, but by twelve, she only painted realistic still lifes that could win church art contests. I watched her imagination retreat behind acceptable expression, just as mine had."

He paused, emotion constricting his throat. "And Judith—we used to hike together. Just the two of us. There was this moment on a mountain ridge when she turned to me, wild-haired in the wind, and said, 'I feel closest to God out here.' Now she sits in the third pew every Sunday, eyes forward, perfectly still. I wonder if she remembers that feeling at all."

Tomkins rose from his chair, unable to contain his energy, and began pacing in a tight circle. He continued, his voice carrying a zeal that demanded attention. "When we deny our genuine emotional responses, we not only diminish our own experience—we reduce what's possible for those around us, too."

His hands shaped invisible forms in the air as if molding the concepts he described. "Our emotional suppression becomes a template for others, particularly those who look to you for guidance."

Phoenix's shoulders slumped as the implication became clear. His gaze drifted to the floor, where he studied the intricate pattern of the wood grain. His emotional amputation hadn't harmed him alone; it had influenced his children, his employees, and his fellow church members. The weight of this realization settled in his chest.

"There's good news," Tomkins added, stopping abruptly in his pacing. He dropped to one knee beside Phoenix's chair, bringing their eyes level. His fingers drummed excitedly on the armrest, and his eyes brightened with the enthusiasm of a man about to share a profound discovery.

Phoenix looked up, a cautious hope flickering across his features.

"The same contagion works in reverse." Tomkins rose again, his movements quick and bird-like. He spread his arms wide, encompassing the entire room. "When you allow yourself authentic emotional expression—tempered by wisdom, not suppressed by fear—you create the capacity for others to do the same."

He tapped his own chest, then motioned toward Phoenix. "Your joy permits their joy. Your appropriate anger validates theirs." His voice softened briefly. "Your willingness to experience shame without being defined by it offers them the same possibility."

He spread his arms wide. "It's revolutionary, Phoenix. Not just for you, but for everyone in your orbit."

Exploring this feeling, Phoenix envisioned the weight of responsibility and the lightness of potential liberation. "How do I start?" he asked, the question emerging from a place of genuine desire.

"Ask what the emotion is telling you," Tomkins replied. Fear might say, 'This situation needs more information before proceeding.' Excitement might say, 'This path has potential worth exploring.'" He pitched closer, his face animated with enthusiasm. "Emotions are messengers, Phoenix. Stop shooting them as they arrive at your door."

Phoenix's facial muscles shifted, relaxing almost imperceptibly, as he considered how different his life might be if he approached emotions as information, not threats.

"We've created cultures that prize rationality over emotionality, that treat feelings as embarrassing disruptions, not essential information." His expression got more serious. "Here's what I discovered after decades of research, Phoenix: emotions aren't the opposite of intelligence—they're a form of intelligence. I believe the most important form." He tapped his head, then his chest. "This and this, working together. Magnificent when it happens."

He motioned toward the books Phoenix had already explored with Beatrix and Pauline. "Intellectual curiosity without emotional engagement becomes sterile academicism. Sensuality without emotional awareness becomes mere thrill-seeking. Spirituality without emotional authenticity becomes empty ritual—ceremony without meaning."

Tomkins provided the connective tissue between mind and body, thought and sensation, and experience and meaning. Phoenix understood now why this conversation had needed to follow the others.

"I can see this will take practice," Phoenix acknowledged. "Decades of patterns don't change overnight."

"Indeed not," Tomkins agreed enthusiastically. "Think of it as physical therapy for the emotional body. Small movements, gradually expanded, eventually restoring the full range of mobility." He finally paused long enough to enjoy a quick taste of his beverage. His face lit up with pleasure.

"I'm willing to try," Phoenix said. "To pay attention differently than I have before."

"The path isn't easy," Tomkins acknowledged, quickly taking another sip as his form faded, as Beatrix's and Pauline's had before their departures. "Changing emotional patterns requires consistent attention. You'll make mistakes and fall back into old scripts."

"There will be days when the critical voices in your head crescendo like a symphony of negativity." He conducted this imaginary symphony with exaggerated gestures. "Yet with practice, you can write new stories where all your emotions have valid roles. Fascinating, complex stories worthy of a person as multidimensional as you!"

Phoenix wanted to ask more questions, to prolong this uncommon conversation, but he could see that familiar haziness returning—the signal that this visitation was nearing its end.

"Remember," Tomkins said, his voice remaining clear despite his increasingly translucent appearance. "Emotions aren't your enemies. They're messengers delivering vital information about what matters to you, what threatens you, and what nourishes you. Honor them as such, and they'll guide you toward a more integrated life than you've ever imagined possible."

He tapped his temple one last time. "The mind may forget, but the body always remembers. Trust it." Tomkins' final words hung in the air as his form dispersed into particles of light that reminded Phoenix of dust motes dancing in sunbeams.

oooo

As Tomkins faded from view, Phoenix discovered the same heaviness descending over him—not unpleasant but insistent, like the approach of sleep after intensive learning. His last thought, before drifting off, was clear: emotions such as curiosity and sensuality were not enemies to be conquered but allies to be embraced.

When he closed his eyes, Phoenix became aware of a quiet resonance in the air around him. It began as a single, pure tone—barely perceptible, like a crystal glass humming at the edge of hearing. The note lingered, sustained beyond what seemed possible, before being joined by a second tone that harmonized perfectly with the first.

As his consciousness hovered in this liminal space, more tones emerged, each adding complexity to the surrounding harmonic structure. The sounds didn't come from any specific direction but seemed to emanate from the room, as if the air molecules were vibrating in orchestrated patterns.

Different tones rose and fell in intensity, creating a composition that seemed to respond to his emotional state. The harmonics shifted from major to minor as his thoughts drifted through Silvan's revelations—moments of joy brightening the tones, fragments of remembered pain deepening them.

These vibrations weren't merely auditory—they traveled through his body, resonating in his chest, fingertips, even his bones. The leather chair beneath him seemed to conduct rather than dampen this vibrational symphony, connecting him more deeply to the experience.

Phoenix sensed that this wasn't a random sound but a form of communication, the room translating complex emotional states into audible frequencies. The manuscript on affect theory resting in his lap began to move, its pages fluttering in response to the tones in the melody.

Gradually, the harmonics coalesced around a central frequency with an ancient quality—something that suggested emotional depth and historical richness as if the vibrations connected him to times long past. The symphony began incorporating what sounded like distant echoes of Renaissance lutes, Medieval chants, and even older rhythms that stirred something primal in his consciousness.

As the sonority deepened, Phoenix became aware of a distinct fragrance emerging—aged sandalwood mingling with rare oud and hints of Moroccan saffron. The scent materialized directly from the harmonics, as if the vibrations were transposing from sound to smell.

The room's dimensions adjusted in response to the vibrations, not changing size but somehow altering perception—corners softened, distances expanded and contracted with the pulse of the harmonics. The experience elicited a measureless sense of timelessness, as if the space were transmuting to accommodate centuries rather than moments.

When Phoenix gradually returned to wakefulness, he noticed the quality of illumination in the circular room had changed again, and the starry night above had fluctuated to layered indigo, casting the sanctum in a dreamlike luminescence that reminded him of twilight in Mediterranean countries—that magical moment when day and night are perfectly balanced. The air seemed imbued with memory, carrying cedar fragrances, aged parchment, and —an essence more elusive—primordial time.

Unlike his previous awakenings, Phoenix experienced no disorientation this time. Instead, he enjoyed a sense of being more fully present. Each breath appeared significant, and each weight shift in the leather chair registered with newfound lucidity. His emotional state, too, seemed more accessible to him—a complex blend of interest, excitement, and enjoyment.

"The body remembers what the mind forgets," came a familiar voice, rich with wisdom and the faint traces of an accent Phoenix had come to recognize.

# Interlude - Mircea

Turning, Phoenix saw Mircea seated not in the chair opposite but on an intricately carved wooden stool near the bar. The older man arranged small glasses on a pewter tray; his movements were measured yet flowing, containing no wasted energy. He wore the same impeccably tailored suit as earlier, but had removed his jacket and rolled his sleeves to the elbow.

His eyes studied Phoenix with evident satisfaction. "You have been on a significant journey," Mircea observed, lifting the tray and approaching. "I must say, you've navigated these waters with exceptional openness. Not everyone who enters this room proves as receptive."

"It's been ... revelatory," Phoenix proclaimed, surprised by the depth of comfort he sensed in the man's company as if they had known each other for decades.

Mircea's smile deepened, genuine pleasure illuminating his features. "Please, tell me what you've discovered thus far."

Deliberating on the question, Phoenix gathered his thoughts. "Beatrix reminded me that curiosity isn't childish but essential—that questions can deepen true understanding. Pauline showed me that my body isn't my enemy—that pleasure can be spiritual, not shameful. Silvan revealed that my emotions aren't weaknesses but messengers—that feeling fully is part of living fully."

"Beautifully articulated," Mircea responded, placing the tray on the table beside him. It held three tiny glasses containing a colored aperitif—ruby, amber, and a transparent liqueur.

Phoenix sighed, feeling understood in a comforting way.

Mircea continued, "Each encounter has begun restoring fragments of your wholeness. Parts of yourself you had been taught to deny or suppress. Integration is like restoring a shattered mirror. Each piece reflects something true, but only together do they show the whole image."

Phoenix thought of his fragments: the businessman, the father, the secret lover, the closeted philosopher. "And if some pieces seem to conflict?"

"Perhaps they only appear to conflict because we're viewing them separately," Mircea suggested. "Step back far enough, and contradictions often reveal themselves as complementary."

"Would you join me in a small ritual?" Mircea asked, indicating the glasses. "A way to honor what has awakened within you?"

With an enthusiastic nod, Phoenix assented.

Mircea lifted the first small glass—the ruby drink—and handed it to Phoenix. "The first integration," he said. "Mind and curiosity. Beatrix's gift to you."

This drink was bright on Phoenix's palate—aromas of berries and spices, with a clarity that seemed to sharpen his thoughts without narrowing them. He found himself aware of questions forming and unfolding in his consciousness, not with the anxious urgency he usually associated with uncertainty but with a pleasurable sense of exploration.

"The second integration," Mircea continued, offering the amber-colored glass. "Body and sensuality. What Pauline awakened in you."

He sipped the drink tentatively, finding it reminiscent of honey and wood smoke, with complex undertones he couldn't identify. It heated him from within, bringing increased sensation to his body.

"The third," Mircea said, handing him the final glass with the clear, shimmering liqueur. "Soul and emotion. What Silvan revealed to you."

Phoenix expected intensity, given the pattern of the previous drinks. Instead, this mixture was intricate, simple at first contact, then expanding into noticeable complexity. It triggered an elevated awareness of the emotional currents already flowing through him—the interest, excitement, and enjoyment he had noticed upon awakening.

"These three integrations," Mircea said, "are only the beginning. Necessary foundations, but not the complete structure."

"There's more?" Phoenix asked, though he already knew the answer. The book by John O'Donohue was still waiting on the table nearby.

"There is always more. That is the nature of true transformation."

Settling deeper into the chair, Phoenix savored the complex flavors of the three integration drinks still lingering on his palate. Mircea's timeless eyes studied him with appreciation.

After a moment, Mircea's gaze drifted around the room, taking in the priceless artifacts and impossible treasures. "You see my collection," he said with a hand encompassing the space. Over centuries, I've witnessed economic systems rise and fall: feudalism, mercantilism, industrial capitalism, and now this curious phase your generation inhabits—where wealth increasingly derives not from creating value but from manipulating abstract symbols."

Phoenix's attention sharpened. "You mean the financial markets?"

"Among other things." Mircea's face held ancient knowledge. "I've accumulated wealth through many systems, but I've observed how each eventually reaches a point where it begins to consume what it once nurtured. Your capitalism once liberated human creativity from rigid hierarchies. Now it increasingly captures and encloses what should remain free—ideas, beauty, time, human connection, even the spiritual."

He lifted one of the empty crystal glasses, examining how it caught the light. "The true perversion of your era isn't wealth itself, but the inversion of means and ends. Markets were created to serve human flourishing. Now humans are evaluated by how well they serve markets."

His voice carried no judgment, only the perspective of one who had witnessed countless civilizations. "I collect these objects not as investments or status symbols, but as containers of meaning. The difference is crucial."

The pursuit of success appeared in a new light, revealing how wealth accumulation had overtaken Phoenix, displacing the meaningful life it was supposed to enable. "What's the alternative?" he asked.

"Remember that economies exist within larger systems—ecological, social, cultural—and when economic values dominate these realms, something essential withers," Mircea replied. The ever-present scent of his cologne —oud and saffron—intensified as he spoke, an ancient fragrance from forgotten markets.

Phoenix looked down at the hands that had built a business empire from nothing. "I've watched that withering in myself, I think."

"The wiser civilizations I've observed understood that markets make excellent servants but tyrannical masters." Mircea's voice carried centuries of observation, though his face remained timeless.

"Like Renaissance Florence?" Phoenix asked the question emerging from half-remembered art history classes.

Mircea inclined his head in affirmation. "In Renaissance Florence, they celebrated commerce but prohibited banking on holy days." His fingers traced an invisible boundary in the air. "The Bhutanese have begun measuring Gross National Happiness alongside GDP."

Phoenix pondered this alternative metric, which was so foreign to the quarterly-driven capitalism he practiced.

"These societies placed boundaries around commercial activity," Mircea continued, his cufflinks catching the ambient light. "They recognized that family bonds, artistic creation, and spiritual practice cannot be reduced to monetary value without destroying their essence."

A memory surfaced—a strategy meeting where "corporate culture" was assigned a numerical value on spreadsheets.

Mircea's eyes held ancient wisdom. "Your business acumen isn't inherently corrupting." The assurance, coming from this ageless presence, carried unexpected weight.

"The question is whether it serves your humanity or diminishes it." Mircea's gaze grew more intense, penetrating beyond surface thoughts. "Whether it expands possibility or narrows it to only what can be measured in currency."

Understanding dawned on Phoenix: his business success, like his family commitment, had been both a gift and a constraint. "I've never thought about it that way."

"Few do," Mircea acknowledged. "The most insidious prisons are those we cannot see. Your economic system, like the modern nuclear family, becomes dangerous the moment it claims there is no alternative—when it presents itself as natural law rather than human creation."

He leaned back a little, studying Phoenix. "I must confess, I'm delighted by your progress. Many who enter this room resist what it offers—they cling to their fragmentation as if it were a virtue."

"It hasn't been easy," Phoenix revealed.

"The most worthwhile journeys rarely are," Mircea replied. "You've shown an incredible willingness to question what you've been taught, to reconsider what you've accepted as immutable truth." There was genuine admiration in his voice. "That is rarer than you might imagine."

Pride warmed his chest at Mircea's words. Then came a eureka moment—where once such praise would have triggered immediate denial or self-deprecation, now he received it, neither inflating nor diminishing its significance.

"What comes next?" Phoenix asked.

"The final integration," Mircea said, his gaze drifting momentarily to the O'Donohue book. "Spirit and freedom." His expression softened and turned almost reverent. "The recognition that the spiritual isn't somewhere else—some distant heaven or remote state of perfection. It's here, in the questioning, sensuality, and emotional human experience."

Responding before thinking, Phoenix said, "My church would label that false teaching."

"Most institutions fear what they cannot control," Mircea said without judgment. "And nothing is less controllable than genuine freedom." He made a slight, elegant movement that encompassed the entire room. "The greatest mistake of many religions is teaching people to deny their humanity instead of fully inhabiting it. As if the cosmos created bodies as obstacles when they are vehicles for experiencing the wonder of existence."

Phoenix considered the dualism inherent in his religious tradition—the constant struggle against "fleshly desires," the valorization of spirit over body, and the suspicion of physical pleasure. How differently might he have lived if taught to honor his embodied nature?

"I've spent my life trying to subjugate my body," he confessed, "to rise above its needs, its desires, its limitations."

"How has that served you?" Mircea asked, not unkindly.

Phoenix knew the answer immediately: that approach had fostered fragmentation rather than wholeness, bred dissociation instead of mindfulness, and rewarded performance over authenticity. "Not well," he acknowledged.

"Not all boundaries are prisons," Mircea observed. "Some create spiritual space. The question is whether they serve life or merely control it."

"There is another way," Mircea said gently. "One that your final visitor will illuminate more fully than I can." He looked around at the circular room with its treasures.

"This collection represents centuries of human wisdom, beauty, and exploration. Yet all of it—every book, every painting, every philosophical insight—emerged through embodied experience. Through hands that wrote, eyes that saw, hearts that felt."

He rose from his chair with that contained energy Phoenix had observed earlier, moving to stand near the center of the circular room where the constellations seemed most concentrated.

"The path ahead," Mircea said, his voice more mellow, "invites you to recognize that spirituality isn't an escape from your humanity but the full, conscious embracing of it. Not denial but acceptance. Not fragmentation but wholeness."

The conclusion of this singular experience filled Phoenix with a mixture of anticipation and grief. "What happens afterward?" he asked. "When I leave this place?"

Mircea's eyes held his with gentle kindness. "That depends entirely on you. Many have passed through this room. Some return to their lives unchanged, treating what they've experienced as an interesting dream or hallucination. Others attempt to apply what they've learned through force of will, creating new forms of the same old fragmentation."

He moved closer, again lightly placing a hand on Phoenix's arm, the aromas of Mircea's unique cologne washing over him. "A few—those who truly understand—recognize that transformation is not a thing to achieve but to embody. They don't try to remember the teachings; they become them. Their way of existing in the world shifts not because they follow new rules but because they live from a different center."

The hand on Phoenix's arm was meaningful, like a blessing given physical form. "Which will you be?" Mircea asked, though his tone suggested it wasn't a question requiring an answer.

"You're learning so much," Mircea observed with evident pleasure. "Remember what I've shared—spiritual freedom begins in the body, not despite it." He moved away and faded from view.

oooo

Instead of passivity overtaking him, Phoenix felt a strange urge to move. He stood, his body responding to an instinct he couldn't name. He picked up the manuscript on affect theory, but as he stepped toward the center of the circular room, he felt it growing lighter, transforming.

Taking another step, he noticed something extraordinary—the constellations above shifted, following his movement. He stopped, staring upward in wonder. The star pattern above him seemed to wink once, as if acknowledging his attention.

Experimentally, Phoenix took a step to the right. The entire celestial display moved with him, maintaining its position directly overhead. He stepped left—again, the stars followed, like an astronomical shadow.

"Impossible," he whispered, a smile of childlike wonder spreading across his face. He took three quick steps forward—the constellations matched his pace perfectly, never losing their alignment with his position.

Understanding dawned—the room responded to him, not merely displaying a passive light show. For the first time since entering the Purging Room, Phoenix felt himself becoming an active participant in its mystery rather than simply its witness.

A playful impulse overtook him. He began to move more deliberately, testing the relationship between his body and the celestial display. He turned in a slow circle—the stars rotated with him. He moved backward—they followed. He extended his hand upward and gasped as several stars brightened in response, as if reaching back.

Growing bolder, knowing he was alone, Phoenix began to dance—not with any formal steps but with the spontaneous movement of someone rediscovering joy in his body. He spun, swayed, and reached outward with expansive gestures. The constellations responded to each movement, creating a cosmic choreography. Stars streaked and swirled, forming luminous trails that lingered momentarily before resolving into new patterns.

"Follow your curiosity," Beatrix had encouraged.

"Trust your body," he remembered Pauline saying.

"Honor your emotions," Silvan had taught.

The three voices harmonized in his memory as Phoenix continued his celestial dance. He felt simultaneously powerful and humble—a conductor of cosmic forces yet also a participant in something far more significant than himself.

As his movements became more fluid and instinctive, the stars began to organize themselves into new configurations. No longer random patterns, they formed recognizable shapes—spirals, knots, and interwoven lines that seemed vaguely familiar.

Phoenix slowed his dance, his attention caught by these emerging forms. He realized they were Celtic patterns—ancient symbols of interconnection and eternal cycles. Triquetra, spirals, and complex knotwork materialized in starlight above him, rotating slowly like a vast cosmic mobile.

Drawn to the center of the room as if by gravitational pull, Phoenix stood with arms extended, turning slowly in place—the star patterns responded by spiraling inward, concentrating their light in a gentle vortex above him. The book in his hands completed its transformation. Where Tomkins' manuscript had been, he now held a much newer book.

Its heft felt solid in his hands. *Anam Cara* was a hardcover with a dust jacket featuring an intricate Celtic knot pattern in muted greens and blues that seemed to alchemize in the room's ethereal light. The title stood prominently across the top in an elegant serif font, with *A Book of Celtic Wisdom* beneath it in smaller lettering.

The book was obviously cherished—its spine showed gentle creases from multiple readings, and the pages frayed slightly at the edges. Opening the cover, Phoenix discovered an inscription in flowing, poetic handwriting: "*To Mircea—For the threshold crossings you've witnessed and guided. May you always find yourself accompanied on the journey. With gratitude, John O'Donohue, Connemara, 1997.*"

The personal dedication made this first edition rare and irreplaceable—a testament to some prior connection between Mircea and the Irish poet-philosopher.

The celestial display began to rain down tiny motes of light that settled on his skin like flickering snowflakes before fading. Each point of contact left a sensation—not of heat or cold, but of connection, as if ancient wisdom was transferred directly through his skin.

The air around him changed, carrying the scent of wild thyme, sea salt, and peat smoke. Phoenix turned, following the fragrance and the stars' pull that continued tracking his movement. As he completed his turn, he was suddenly facing a weathered man with kind eyes and mud on his boots.

"In the Celtic tradition," came a melodious voice touched with a lilting Irish brogue, "we understand that a book is more than paper and ink. It's a gateway between worlds, a conversation waiting to happen. Between its covers, a wee bit of magic always hides. When you have hundreds of ancient books, the magic increases exponentially, and these phenomena can occur."

The constellations made one final adjustment, aligning themselves perfectly above Phoenix and his new visitor, as if blessing the encounter that was about to unfold.

# CHAPTER EIGHT

## Celtic Freedom

He appeared in his early fifties, when he smiled his eyes crinkled at the corners. His thick hair was touched with gray at the temples, and his face held the weathered lines of someone who had spent countless hours in conversation with both the elements and the cosmos.

He wore a simple dark sweater and corduroy trousers, not clerical garb. Yet, there was an unmistakable priestliness in his spirit—not in the sense of religious authority, but in the older meaning of one who tends sacred fires.

"*Dia dhuit, a* Phoenix. I'm John O'Donohue. Your name speaks of transformation through fire—perhaps our most ancient wisdom." He reached out his hand.

A firm handshake, and then, "Mr. O'Donohue," Phoenix said softly, feeling no surprise at this final visitation, only a sense of rightness, of completion. He again noticed the mud on O'Donohue's boots and a small tear in the elbow of his sweater—signs of a man who inhabited the physical world fully despite his philosophical depth.

"Indeed, *a chara*, please call me John," he replied, the Gaelic term of endearment flowing naturally from his tongue. "Though names are temporary addresses for the mystery each of us embodies, aren't they?" His voice had an unhurried rhyme, words flowing with the natural meter of poetry even in ordinary speech.

"This book," holding up Phoenix's mystical chronicle, "Could only have been conceived by the ancient Celts," he winked, "...or by Mircea. Amazing!"

"I see you've been on quite the journey since entering this room. A pilgrimage moving from the outer circles toward the center."

Seeing no need to explain or justify himself to this gentle presence, Phoenix said, "It's been transformative."

"Yes, transformation," O'Donohue's eyes lit up, his face animating with genuine delight. "The only constant in a universe of change, yet the thing we humans resist most fiercely. Like trying to hold back the tide with a bucket and spade."

John sat down, carefully laid Phoenix's chronicle on the side table, and reached for the drink beside it. With a signal, he invited Phoenix to join him and take up his glass, another new cocktail Dion had created for this encounter.

"*Slàinte mhath na h-anam!*" John raised his glass. "Which means good health of the soul! May you find the courage to listen to your heart, the wisdom to hear the ancient whispers of this place, and the grace to recognize the spiritual presence that dwells within the ordinary moments of life."

They drank deeply, savoring the exquisite Irish whiskey with its perfect balance of sweet, sour, and botanical elements.

"Now that's soul nectar," John said, wiping his mouth with the back of his hand in a gesture more reminiscent of a farmer than a philosopher-priest. He angled his body, his gaze direct but kind. "Tell me, Phoenix—because names matter, and yours is particularly apt—what have you discovered about freedom in your conversations here?"

The question reverberated in the circular room as if the cosmos were repeating it. Phoenix took a moment to gather his thoughts, acutely aware that O'Donohue was inviting him to articulate what he'd experienced.

"I've discovered that I've been caged," he began slowly, "not by external constraints but by beliefs I've internalized so deeply that I've stopped seeing them as beliefs at all." He indicated the chair where his previous visitors had sat. "Beatrix revealed how I've confined my mind. Pauline showed me how I've imprisoned my body. Silvan illuminated how I've restricted my emotions."

"All in the name of a god who supposedly created these aspects of your humanity," O'Donohue observed, with no judgment in his tone, only compassion. "Sure, isn't that the great paradox? The 'divine' gives us these gifts, and then we're taught to mistrust them."

"When I was a boy in Connemara," O'Donohue responded, his eyes crinkling with understanding, "my father sent me to bring the cows home through a dense fog. I was terrified, sure I'd be lost forever." He mimed a child's wide-eyed fear, then chuckled. "Instead of following the path, I followed the smell of the animals, the sound of their bells. That was my first lesson in trusting senses beyond sight."

He leaned forward. "What you're describing, Phoenix, is learning to navigate the fog of societal expectations by trusting your deeper senses, just as I learned to trust more than my eyes that day."

This glimpse of O'Donohue's childhood drew in Phoenix. He saw the boy beneath the man and recognized how perfectly the story illuminated his life journey.

John shook his head, a rueful grin playing on his lips. His speech had a hypnotic quality and pacing, deliberate pauses that allowed meaning to unfold and settle in Phoenix's mind. He radiated wisdom and trustworthiness.

"When did you first feel the divine as restrictive rather than liberating?" O'Donohue asked, his eyes attentive.

oooo

Phoenix remembered Sunday School at age eight, the flannel board with smiling Jesus surrounded by children. "Jesus loves you when you're good," the teacher had explained. Then, the flip side—flames, red and orange felt pieces arranged to suggest hell. "This is where people who don't obey go." He'd had nightmares for weeks, imagining flames licking at his feet every time he did wrong.

oooo

"I was eight," Phoenix said. "They used heaven and hell as behavior management tools. I started seeing God as a scorekeeper rather than a father."

"*A chara*," O'Donohue sighed, "What a tragedy to turn cosmic mystery into divine surveillance."

"There was a revival when I was fifteen—an emotional multi-night church event aimed at spiritual recommitment," Phoenix continued, the memory surfacing unexpectedly.

"The speaker had us close our eyes and told us to imagine Jesus standing before us, disappointed in our sins. 'Look at his face,' the man had urged, voice breaking with feigned emotion. 'See how you've hurt him.' I remember praying desperately, 'I'm sorry, I'm sorry,' though I wasn't sure for what. I felt inadequate, convinced I could never be good enough."

"And so the sacred became a source of shame rather than wonder," O'Donohue observed sadly. "They turned the cosmic embrace into a prison cell, didn't they? Sure, isn't that the great blasphemy—reducing spiritual mystery to a tiny box built of human fear?"

He leaned back for a time, looking at Phoenix with eyes that seemed to hold ancient knowledge. "There's an unfathomable violence in that kind of spiritual practice— a violence turned against the self in the name of holiness." He repositioned in his chair, making himself more comfortable.

His expression darkened momentarily, then cleared as he reached for his drink again. "Reminds me of the old priest in our village when I was a boy—Father Brennan, fierce man with eyebrows like wild hedges." John's open hands moved expressively, sketching the imposing eyebrows in the air. "He'd pound the pulpit every Sunday, describing God's wrath in such detail you'd think he and the Almighty shared their morning tea."

John chuckled, the sound warm despite the subject. "One Sunday, during a tremendous thunderstorm, lightning struck the church bell tower. Right in the middle of Father Brennan's most fearsome description of divine punishment. The whole congregation gasped—surely God was emphasizing the priest's point."

His eyes twinkled with mischief. "But old Mrs. Sullivan, who'd buried three husbands and feared neither God nor man, stood right up and announced, 'Perhaps the Almighty is tired of getting misrepresented, Father.' Ha! It was the first time I ever considered that God might have a sense of humor."

Phoenix found himself smiling at the image. "Unfortunately, my church would call Mrs. Sullivan's life experience false doctrine," Phoenix said, though without the certainty such a statement would have carried days earlier.

O'Donohue laughed, the sound ardent and genuine, filling the room with earnestness. "For the love of all that's holy! These labels we're so fond of—pagan, Christian, false doctrine, heretical. Sure, doesn't the cosmic mystery itself laugh at our wee attempts to contain it in categories? Grand foolishness, that."

John reached for his glass, which was mysteriously full again, "The ancient Celts were spiritual for centuries before Christianity arrived on our shores. They retained an understanding of spirituality deeply connected to the natural world, the body, and the cycles of existence. They saw no contradiction between worshipping a god and honoring the spiritual in the turn of the seasons, in the curve of a woman's hip, and in asking difficult questions."

He took a sip, the amber whiskey glistening like diamonds. "They understood that the cosmos speaks many languages, not just one."

"Again, my programming comes out," Phoenix stated. "That sounds dangerously close to relativism; if everything is sacred, then nothing is. Don't we need boundaries, definitions?"

"Do we?" O'Donohue asked gently. "Or have we been taught to need them because we fear the vastness of mystery? Is a rainbow less beautiful for having no clear boundary between its colors?"

Frowning, Phoenix asked, "But without clear guidance, how do we know right from wrong? What prevents chaos?"

"Maybe the question isn't what prevents chaos," O'-Donohue suggested, "but what prevents love? What hinders our ability to recognize the spiritual in ourselves and others?" He looked at the book in Phoenix's hands. "Do you know what *anam cara* means?"

Phoenix shook his head.

"Soul friend," O'Donohue translated, the words emerging with layered meaning. "In Celtic spirituality, an *anam cara* is one with whom you can share your innermost self, withholding nothing. One who sees you completely and loves what they see."

His voice softened. "Tell me now, when was the last time you were fully seen and fully loved, Phoenix? Not for your achievements or how well you minded the rules, no —but for your authentic, complex, contradictory self? A long time it's been, hasn't it?"

The question pierced Phoenix with unexpected force. He regarded his marriage to Prudence as characterized by mutual artifice instead of candid sharing. His relationship with his daughters filtered through the expectations of his religious community. Of his affair with Lilith, which came closest to this ideal but remained compartmentalized, separate from the rest of his life.

"I'm not sure," he confessed, the realization somehow both painful and liberating.

"*Mo chroí*," O'Donohue said, the Gaelic term of sympathy flowing naturally from him, "The greatest longing of the human heart is to be seen. Not the carefully constructed persona we show to the world, but our true face —the one that includes our shadows as well as our light, our desires as well as our devotions, our questions as well as our certainties."

He pivoted inward, again gazing in silence while holding Phoenix's eyes, and then, "Would you not agree that's a fair bit closer to love than mere approval could ever be?"

The truth of these words reverberated throughout the deepest chambers of Phoenix's consciousness. How exhausting it had been to maintain his various masks all these years, how much energy he had poured into ensuring these identities never fully intersected, never contaminated each other. The weight of that constant performance settled in his shoulders, a familiar tension he'd carried for so long he'd stopped noticing it until this moment of recognition.

"Freedom," O'Donohue continued, "begins with this kind of self-recognition—the courageous acknowledgment of all that we are, not only the parts deemed acceptable by family, church, or culture." He looked around the room, somehow encompassing the impossible treasures with a glance.

"What Mircea has created here is out of the ordinary, but not half as extraordinary as what you carry within you —the unique confluence of experiences, perceptions, desires, and capacities that constitute your self." He raised his glass in a salute. "You are not a problem to be solved, Phoenix. You're a mystery to be embraced." They both drank deeply.

Edging closer, John's gaze intensified: "Do you know the most insidious prison, Phoenix? It's the one we build for ourselves through the internalized voices of others: the father who says success is measured in dogmatic terms, the pastor who insists spirituality means suppressing desire, the culture that teaches men to amputate their emotional lives in the name of strength."

He tapped his chin gently. "These voices become the wardens we carry within, and we mistake their judgments for our own. Fierce jailers we become to ourselves, so we do."

These words touched Phoenix physically—gentle yet firm, like skilled hands locating and releasing points of stress he hadn't known he carried. "How do you break free of that?" he asked, the question emerging from a place of genuine need.

O'Donohue smiled, transforming his face into an expression both ancient and youthful. "Not by replacing one set of external authorities with another. Freedom doesn't come from following new rules, even beautiful ones."

He swept his open hand toward the vast collection of books lining the circular room. "All the wisdom ever written amounts to signposts, not destinations. The journey itself must be yours alone. Though," he added with a wink, "that doesn't mean it must be lonely."

He sat back in his chair in silence, his expression becoming more contemplative. After a time, he thoughtfully continued, "There's a wee mountain lake in Connemara I used to visit—fierce stillness it had, so when the winds were quiet, it would mirror the sky above perfectly. A thin place, that lake. Heaven and earth kissing, they were."

His voice was rhythmic, almost hypnotic in its gentle cadence. "That lake taught me a priceless lesson about the human spirit. When we're at rest, undisturbed by the agitations of fear or the compulsions of ego, we naturally reflect the cosmos. Not through effort or achievement, but through simple awareness." He traced a circle on the arm of his chair. "Like water finding its level, the soul naturally seeks its true nature when we stop forcing it into shapes it was never meant to hold."

Contemplating this image, Phoenix felt its resonance with his own experience. How rarely had he allowed himself such stillness and attentiveness? His life had been characterized by constant activity and striving, as if value could only be found in achievement.

"I had a moment once," Phoenix revealed hesitantly. "Years ago, hiking in the mountains alone. Everything seemed ... connected. Not separate parts but a single living whole. It terrified me. I never told anyone about it."

"Oh my," O'Donohue nodded, "a thin place—where the veil between worlds momentarily lifts. And why did it frighten you, do you think?"

"Because it didn't fit," Phoenix said after reflection. "Not with the God I'd been taught to believe in. This was much wilder. Less contained."

"The spiritual, *a chara*, has never been as small as our descriptions of it. Those moments of recognition—sure, aren't they invitations, not aberrations? Mystical whispers they are, calling us home."

Phoenix thought of the quiet moments of genuine transcendence he'd experienced—not in church services but in solitude, in nature, in unexpected kindnesses. Those moments had nothing to do with doctrine and everything to do with presence.

"How do you maintain those moments in the real world?" Phoenix asked, "With responsibilities, relationships, expectations?"

"There's the rub," O'Donohue acknowledged gently. Mud from his boots had left a small mark on the floor—a piece of Ireland transplanted to this magical room. "The modern world conspires against presence. Always pulling us toward the next moment, the next goal, the next acquisition."

"That describes my entire career," Phoenix admitted. "Always focused on the next quarter, the next deal."

"Like a fierce wind that never lets the water settle," O'Donohue said, his hands creating rippling motions between them. The smell of peat and sea salt emanated from his weathered sweater.

"Yes, that's exactly how it feels," Phoenix agreed, "My mind never stops long enough to reflect anything clearly."

O'Donohue scratched his chin thoughtfully, the rasp of stubble audible in the quiet room. "What if presence isn't a quality you maintain but an awareness you return to? Not a permanent state but a practice of homecoming?"

The Celtic knots on the ceiling seemed to weave new patterns as this idea took root.

"Let me tell you about an old farmer I knew growing up," O'Donohue said, his voice taking on the cadence of storytelling. The Irish lilt became more pronounced and musical. "Liam Connolly worked in the same rocky fields his grandfather had cleared."

The air between them thickened with memory, as if the room was leaning in closer to hear the tale.

"Every morning before dawn, he'd walk the boundaries of his land. Not checking fences or looking for problems, though he noticed those too. He was simply greeting his place, as he called it."

A worn path through misty fields materialized in Phoenix's mind, boot prints in dew-covered grass.

John's expression softened, crow's feet deepening around his eyes. "I asked him once why he did this, rain or shine, even in his eighties, when walking pained him."

He paused, marking the moment. "'A place needs to be recognized,' he told me, 'and a man needs to remember he belongs somewhere.'"

The words landed with unexpected weight. When was the last time Phoenix had felt he truly belonged anywhere?

"That was his spiritual practice," O'Donohue finished softly, "though he'd never have called it that. Recognizing and belonging—daily acts of return."

Phoenix's breathing synchronized with O'Donohue's, creating an intimate and spacious shared rhythm. As his breath deepened, he was aware of sensations in his body —the gentle expansion of his rib cage, the slight air across his upper lip, and the gradual relaxation of his stomach muscles.

"You're experiencing it now," O'Donohue observed, his words soft with appreciation. "This is *beannacht*—a blessing. It is not conferred from outside but recognized within. The Celtic understanding of blessing isn't about invoking divine favor but acknowledging the spiritual existing in each moment, breath, and sensation. It's not begging for salvation from punishment but recognizing that we're already soaked to the skin with goodness."

Closing his eyes, Phoenix envisioned fully experiencing this simple yet blissful state. When he opened them again, he found O'Donohue watching him with gentle approval.

"Your evangelical tradition often speaks of salvation only happening once, a singular moment of commitment. The Celtic understanding is different—awakening as ongoing revelation, a continuous unfolding of the spiritual within the ordinary." He traced another circle. "Not a straight line leading to a distant heaven, but a spiral dance that brings us ever closer to the center while embracing ever wider circles of understanding."

Phoenix recalled his conversion experience decades earlier—a moment of emotional ardor at a youth retreat that had set the course of his spiritual life. How different might his journey have been if he'd understood faith not as a fixed destination but as a continuing exploration?

"In your tradition," O'Donohue observed, "pleasure is often viewed with suspicion—a distraction from spiritual concerns at best, a temptation toward sin at worst." His expression held a gentle reproof. "What if pleasure is itself a form of connection to the universe? A way of saying 'yes' to the gift of embodied existence? Sure, what else would the senses be for—if not to experience the wonder of life?"

He shook his head as if puzzled by the notion. "Strange theology that sees divine creation and then calls it threatening."

O'Donohue chuckled, a warm sound that invited Phoenix to share the humor. "Ah, reminds me of Father Dolan, who used to lecture us in the seminary about 'mortification of the flesh.' There he'd be, all fire and brimstone about denying bodily pleasures, while smoking one of the fine cigars his sister would send him. One day, I asked him why smoking wasn't considered a sinful pleasure."

John laughed outright at the memory. "The poor man nearly choked on his cigar! He sputtered, 'That's different—it helps me think.' We all have our exceptions to our own rules, don't we? Those pleasures we convince ourselves don't count because we enjoy them too much to give them up."

The question reinforced Phoenix's encounter with Pauline Réage, how she had guided him to experience forbidden physical pleasure as life-giving. "I've never thought of it that way," he affirmed.

"The body knows things the mind has forgotten," O'Donohue said, echoing a theme of the evening. "In Celtic understanding, there was never a division between the physical and spiritual realms—only a thin place, a membrane through which the mystical and ordinary constantly intermingle."

Again, Phoenix divined the truth of these words resonating through his consciousness. How differently he might have lived if he'd understood his body not as an obstacle to spiritual growth but as its vehicle. "I've spent my life trying to rise above my humanity," he confessed. "To be less emotional, less physical, less … messy."

O'Donohue's laugh was warm and genuine. "Oh, but the cosmos loves mess. Look at the universe—no straight lines, only spirals and cycles, expansions and contractions, deaths that become births." His eyes sparkled. "What if spiritual freedom isn't found beyond our humanity but through it, not despite our desires, questions, and emotions, but in their midst? The cosmos seems far more comfortable with complexity than we are."

He reached out and gently tapped Phoenix's knee. "I once buried a young woman who died in childbirth, leaving behind a husband mad with grief. At the wake, he got roaring drunk and started cursing God with language that would make a sailor blush. The other mourners were scandalized, wanting to remove him."

John's face softened with the memory. "I stopped them. 'Leave him be,' I told them. 'His rage is the purest prayer in this room.'"

Your tradition misses the point—that even our anger, confusion, and despair can be pathways to the divine when expressed honestly rather than buried beneath polite pretense. Silvan could explain this better.

This perspective was entirely different from what Phoenix had been taught, and he was momentarily disoriented as if familiar landmarks had transferred position.

"My apologies, but I keep returning to this question: Without clear borders and rules, doesn't everything become relative? How do you know what's right?"

"A fair question," O'Donohue acknowledged, nodding appreciatively. "Consider this: what's 'right' isn't a fixed set of prohibitions but a way of living in relationship—with yourself, with others, with the world around you." He canted closer. "In Celtic spirituality, the greatest sin isn't breaking the rules but breaking connection—treating others or yourself as objects, as means to an end rather than mysteries to be reverenced."

He touched the book in Phoenix's hands. "*Anam cara* —soul friendship—begins with becoming a friend to your soul, treating all aspects of yourself with the same compassion you would offer a beloved friend. Can you imagine speaking to someone you deeply care about the same way you've spoken to yourself for decades? Dismissing their desires as corrupt? Belittling their questions as dangerous? Judging their emotions as weak?"

He shook his head, "Fierce cruel we can be to ourselves in ways we'd never dream of doing to another, isn't that the truth of it?"

Phoenix couldn't imagine treating anyone he loved with such harshness. Yet, he recognized immediately that this was how he had treated himself—policing his thoughts, suppressing his desires, hiding his emotions, all in the name of spiritual discipline.

"The Celtic imagination," O'Donohue continued, "understands that the spiritual doesn't need protection from the sensual. Indeed, the sensual is one of the most boundless expressions of the spirit." His voice took on a more poetic quality.

"Think of how sunlight moves on water, how wind shapes stone over centuries, how the curve of a lover's neck can stop time itself. These aren't distractions from the cosmic mystery but revelations of it—the invisible made visible through the miracle of perception."

As he spoke, Phoenix was aware of yet another unique phenomenon. The stars above were intensifying, not painfully but with a clarity that rendered everything in the room more picturesque, more immediate.

"You're beginning to see with different eyes," O'-Donohue observed, noticing Phoenix's widened gaze. "Not looking but beholding—perceiving the world not as a collection of separate objects but as a living unity in which you participate." His smile deepened. "This is what the Celtic mystics called 'the gaze of love'—the way of seeing that recognizes the spirit in everything it beholds."

It felt as if scales were falling from Phoenix's eyes—not all at once, but gradually, allowing him glimpses of a world more vibrant and interconnected than he had ever imagined. The books lining the walls, the paintings at the cardinal points, even the whiskey cocktail—all seemed charged with significance.

There was another lingering silence, and Phoenix rested in it. "Beauty is not a luxury, Phoenix," O'Donohue said softly, "but a necessity for the spirit. Not mere decoration but a revelation—the cosmos speaking directly to our senses." He swept his gaze toward the impossible treasures surrounding them.

"Mircea understands this. Each object in this collection is a doorway to wonder, to the recognition that reality is far more phenomenal than our limited conceptions of it. Like thresholds between worlds, so they are."

He pointed to his worn boots and the tear in his sweater. "I've never much cared for pristine things myself. The Japanese have a concept called *wabi-sabi*—finding beauty in imperfection, impermanence, and incompleteness. I've always found more grace in weathered stones than polished marble, in faces lined by experience than those artificially smoothed."

As if to demonstrate, O'Donohue ran a hand over his face, with its lines of laughter and contemplation. "Each wrinkle a story, each scar a lesson. The body carries our history, doesn't it? Such honesty in that."

A revelation struck him—how little attention he'd given to beauty and wonder throughout his life. His homes decorated by professionals to project success rather than express joy. Even his reading had been chosen for utility rather than delight. "I've missed a lot," he said, the realization bringing not despair but a growing interest, recognizing possibilities still available.

"Perhaps," O'Donohue acknowledged, "but the Celtic understanding of time offers hope here too. The past is never entirely fixed—it remains open to new interpretations, new meanings."

"Your business world has a different relationship with time than the Celtic understanding," O'Donohue observed, his weathered hands motioning expressively. "Where do you feel this most acutely?"

Phoenix considered the question. "In quarterly earnings calls," he finally said. "Everything—all work, all value—gets compressed into ninety-day cycles. Long-term thinking means five years at most."

"And what happens to projects that might take longer to bear fruit?" O'Donohue asked.

"They're rarely approved unless they can be broken into 'deliverable milestones' with measurable returns at each stage." Phoenix shook his head. "I had a reforestation initiative I wanted our foundation to support. When I mentioned the trees wouldn't mature for decades, the board chair asked, 'What's the quarterly impact story?'"

"Ah," O'Donohue nodded, "the impatience of capitalism meets the patience of nature. Did you know the great medieval cathedrals often took over a century to complete? The stonemasons laying foundations knew that they would never see the spires. Yet they carved each stone with exquisite care."

"That would never survive a modern board meeting," Phoenix said with a wry smile.

"And in your soul, which timeline speaks to you more truthfully?" O'Donohue's eyes held Phoenix's gently. "The quarterly report or the cathedral?"

Phoenix's answer surprised himself. "I've built my success on the first while secretly longing for the second."

"I attended a corporate strategic planning day last month," he continued. "Our consultant had us map business cycles against competitive windows. Four hours in, I stared out the window at an ancient oak tree on the property. It had lived long before our company existed and would remain long after."

"And what did that tree say to you?" O'Donohue asked, smiling.

"That's just it—I felt it was speaking, though I couldn't quite hear the message. When I mentioned this to our CFO during a break, he looked at me like I was hallucinating. 'It's just landscaping, Phoenix,' he said. 'Focus on the five-year projection.'"

"The tree," O'Donohue said gently, "was offering you a glimpse of sacred time—the slow, cyclical unfolding that nourishes deeper meaning. Your business measures time as currency to be spent. The Celtic soul knows time as presence to be experienced."

"In Celtic spirituality, *a chara*, 'enough' is a spiritual concept, so it is. The modern marketplace has no notion of 'enough'—only 'more' and 'not yet enough.' Terrible hunger it creates, that thinking."

O'Donohue reached into his pocket and pulled out a smooth stone, turning it over in his fingers. "I was walking with a successful businessman once—fellow who'd made millions in tech but couldn't sleep at night. We were along the Atlantic coast, and I asked him to pick up a stone from the shore. He chose the largest, most impressive one he could find."

John's eyes twinkled. "I asked him to close his eyes and feel it. 'What's it telling you?' I asked. He looked at me like I'd lost my mind. 'It's a rock, John,' he said. 'It's not telling me anything.' So I picked up a small, ordinary pebble, worn smooth by countless waves. 'This stone,' I told him, 'has existed for millions of years. It will continue long after your company's stock price is forgotten. What might humility feel like in the face of such permanence?'"

John placed the stone on the floor between them. "The man wept, Phoenix. First time in twenty years, he told me later. Not because of anything I said, but because the stone offered him perspective his balance sheets never could."

Again, the truth resounded in Phoenix's whole self. How much of his life had been spent pursuing a "more" that never arrived?

"What if," O'Donohue suggested, "true abundance isn't measured in acquisition but in attention? Not in unlimited growth but in cyclical harmony?"

His eyes held Phoenix's with gentle focus. "Your journey until now hasn't been wasted. Every experience, every choice—even the ones you might now reconsider—has brought you to this moment of awakening. All part of the same beautiful, complex spiral."

The words seemed to enter Phoenix, as if spoken directly to his spirit. He looked up to again find O'Donohue watching him with quiet understanding.

"Trust the indirect, the oblique," O'Donohue intoned. "Your evangelical tradition values certainty, directness, and clear answers to clear questions. But the spirit speaks differently—through dreams, coincidences, unexpected attractions, persistent longings that can't be explained away."

He softened. "These aren't distractions from your path but essential clues to it. Isn't it grand how the universe speaks in whispers we must lean in to hear?"

Phoenix weighed his attraction to Lilith, his persistent questions about faith, and his longing for experiences beyond the narrow confines of his religious community. Were these temptations away from his true path or signposts toward it?

"The geography of your destiny," O'Donohue continued, "isn't mapped through external authorities—not pastors or scriptures or cultural expectations—but through attentiveness to your own deepest nature. Your desires are not random or corrupt but meaningful, pointing toward what your soul needs for its fulfillment." He patted his chest. "The cosmos speaks most clearly not from pulpits but within your longing."

"How do you distinguish between genuine desire and mere selfishness?" Phoenix asked, voicing a concern instilled in him through decades of religious teaching. "Between genuine guidance and self-deception?"

O'Donohue's face acknowledged the legitimacy of the question. "Honest desire brings you more fully alive, capable of paying attention, more available for connection. It expands your capacity for wonder, compassion, and appreciation of beauty."

His expression grew more serious. "Mere selfishness, by contrast, diminishes these qualities—leaving you more isolated, more defended, more committed to maintaining the barriers between yourself and genuine experience."

He waved his arm. "Ask yourself this: Does this choice, this relationship, this belief system make me more available to love or less? More capable of wonder or less? More conscious of the miracle of existence or less? The answers will guide you more certainly than any external authority ever could."

He smiled encouragingly. "True north isn't a point on a map but a resonance within your existence."

Again, Phoenix calculated his marriage, work, and church involvement through this lens. How often had these central commitments left him feeling not more alive but more depleted, not more connected but more isolated, not more mindful but more distracted?

"I've been living against the grain of my nature for a long time," he recognized, the admission painful yet liberating. His hands opened and closed on the armrests, physically showing his mental grasping and release.

"Many do," O'Donohue said gently. He leaned back in his chair, weathered hands resting comfortably on his knees. "Modern life conspires against authenticity. It always pulls us toward conformity, predictability, and the safety of the known rather than the adventure of becoming." His eyes drifted toward the celestial display above, then returned to Phoenix with renewed focus.

Phoenix peered at the floor as he considered his business, successful but achieved by following established patterns, meeting external expectations, and suppressing his creative impulses in favor of proven strategies.

"The spirit," O'Donohue interjected, "thrives in the opposite direction—toward uniqueness, mystery, and the continuous unfolding of potential that can never be fully predicted or controlled. That makes it so fierce and beautiful, wouldn't you say?"

oooo

Phoenix thought of something Lilith had mentioned during their last conversation before his Shanghai trip: "A gallery in Barcelona called. They want to feature my enantiodromia series in a solo exhibition." Pride suffused her voice, and Phoenix felt a complex emotion—joy for her success tinged with the awareness that her life moved forward along its own axis, not orbiting his.

"Will you go?" he'd asked, imagining her in that Spanish city, vibrant and alive among kindred spirits. "I haven't decided," she'd replied, and he'd heard the unspoken question: Would he still be tethered to his old life if she did?

Her ambitions weren't bargaining chips or ultimatums—they were simply hers, claimed without apology. She embodied freedom—the everyday courage of living truthfully in an ordinary world.

oooo

O'Donohue glanced at the full glass beside him, then back to Phoenix with a conspiratorial look. "You know, I've always found it curious that your American churches forbid alcohol, given that in their Bible, Jesus' first miracle was turning water into wine. At a wedding celebration, no less," He chuckled. "Not medicinal wine, mind you. Party wine. The good stuff saved for last."

He inclined towards Phoenix. "And why would that be chosen as a first revelation? Perhaps because joy, celebration, and physical pleasure are not obstacles to spiritual life but expressions of it. Perhaps because a God said to enter creation through human birth understands that embodiment itself is spiritual."

Phoenix nodded, and they both enjoyed a generous quaff. "I've valued certainty over curiosity, security over exploration," he said, thinking about his life, which was successful but achieved by following established patterns, meeting external expectations, and suppressing his creative impulses.

"As have most," O'Donohue replied without judgment. "We're taught from childhood to seek the safety of the known, to distrust the unfamiliar, to value answers over questions." His eyes held a gentle challenge.

He continued, "What if the purpose of life isn't to arrive at certainty but to cultivate wonder? Consider how a child experiences a butterfly, not categorizing its species but marveling at its flight. Not eliminating the mystery of its transformation but delighting in it. Not answering how it navigates, but living in the question of its journey."

O'Donohue's form seemed to disperse as he spoke, becoming less substantial, much like Phoenix's previous visitors had toward the ends of their conversations. Unlike earlier transitions, Phoenix experienced no anxiety about this impending departure—only a peaceful acceptance, a recognition that all encounters, however pure, are temporary.

"I don't know if I can reconcile all of this," Phoenix announced. "My faith, questions, and experiences don't form a coherent picture."

John's eyebrows raised, "What if coherence isn't what is needed? Perhaps it's cohesion, *mo chroí*—allowing all these aspects to exist together, even in their contradictions. The Celtic mind knows this truth well, so it does."

"Your faith itself isn't the prison," O'Donohue clarified. "The longing for connection with something greater —that's as natural as breathing. It's the rigid structures built around that longing, the walls that claim to protect but actually confine, that create suffering."

"I think I want to try," Phoenix said carefully. "Not to have all the answers, but to live the questions more honestly."

"That," O'Donohue said, "is the beginning of real freedom. Not arrival, but setting out on the journey with open eyes.

Before I go," O'Donohue said, his words remaining clear despite his increasingly translucent appearance, "let me offer you what the Celts would call a *beannacht*—a blessing." He extended his arm, his gaze tender. "Not as one with spiritual authority blessing one without, but as one soul recognizing another—*anam cara* to *anam cara*."

John placed a shimmering hand lightly on his book in Phoenix's lap while holding the burgundy chronicle with the other and then spoke in that musical brogue that made even ordinary words sound like poetry. As he began to speak, the room seemed to still, each phrase falling like gentle rain.

"For your awakening soul, I offer this blessing:

May you awaken to the mystery of being here
and enter the quiet immensity of your own
presence.

May you have joy and peace
in the temple of your senses.

May you receive great encouragement when
new frontiers beckon.

May you respond to the call of your gift
and find the courage to follow its path.

May the flame of anger free you from falsity.

May warmth of heart keep your presence aflame
and may anxiety never linger about you.

May your outer dignity reflect
an inner dignity of spirit.

May you take time to celebrate
the quiet miracles that seek no attention.

May you be consoled

in the secret symmetry of your soul.

May you experience each day as a gift
wrapped around the heart of wonder.

And may you come to accept your deepest longings
as spiritual urgency.

*Go raibh síocháin leat.*"

The final words—a traditional Irish blessing meaning "May peace be with you"—seemed to linger in the air even as O'Donohue's form faded, leaving Phoenix alone in the circular room.

oooo

Yet he didn't feel alone. The blessing had created a palpable sense of companionship with O'Donohue and himself. Phoenix was becoming aware of his existence as unique yet connected to everything. The celestial bodies above seemed aurora-like as they illuminated the room with that unusual clarity, revealing the spiritual in the moment.

The silence was vibrant with possibilities not yet realized. Phoenix closed his eyes, embracing this moment of completion and beginning. The journey through the Purging Room had begun to transform him by revealing what had always been available, waiting to be recognized and embraced.

oooo

As he sat in this state of peaceful mindfulness, he was conscious of soft footsteps approaching. Opening his eyes, he saw Dion moving toward him with that gentle grace that seemed otherworldly. Phoenix realized he'd been watching Dion's movements with appreciation throughout the night, a realization that didn't alarm him as it once might have.

"It's time," Dion said, his enchanting face open and welcoming, as he gathered Phoenix's book from the side table, "Mircea will join us before you leave."

Rising with a new awareness of his body's motion, Phoenix glanced again at the four books—Potter, Réage, Tomkins, and O'Donohue—now back and neatly arranged on the side table.

# CHAPTER NINE

## Return Threshold

S trolling around the mystical room one last time, Phoenix sensed yet another unusual phenomenon, as if he were moving through layers of his consciousness. Each step brought a revelation, a resistance, a release, and a reclamation. The impossible treasures of the Purging Room seemed to acknowledge his passing, the rare books, paintings, and spirits bearing witness to his transformation as they had for countless others before him.

Dion moved with that flowing grace Phoenix had recognized—each flex containing spontaneity and inevitability, like water finding its natural course. The young man's persona seemed more defined, as if Phoenix's increased awareness allowed him to perceive Dion more completely. As he moved closer, Dion emitted those now familiar primal aromas: earth after rain, forest floor at dawn.

They paused, looking at the walnut door through which Phoenix had entered the circular room. Dion turned to face him, that fascinating face—neither entirely male nor female, neither young nor ancient—holding his with an expression of genuine fervor.

"The portal works in both directions," Dion said softly. "Crossing it again doesn't erase what you've experienced here, but it does require a different kind of courage."

Phoenix understood. Entering the Purging Room had demanded the courage to confront what he had denied. Leaving would require the courage to embody what he had discovered in the complexities of everyday life. "I'm not sure I know how," Phoenix declared, no shame in the confession.

"None of us do, at first," came Mircea's voice behind them. He had somehow materialized from behind the circular room's bookshelves. "We learn by living the questions, not demanding immediate answers."

Phoenix turned to find the older man approaching. His silver hair caught the reflection, and his movements contained the same regal grace Phoenix had observed earlier. He had donned his jacket again and now appeared as he had during their first meeting—elegantly formal yet utterly at ease.

"Mircea," Phoenix began, then faltered, finding ordinary language inadequate for what he wished to express. How does one thank another for facilitating a rebirth?

Mircea smiled, those caring eyes reflecting understanding. "No gratitude is necessary," he said gently. "What happened here was not given to you but recognized within you. The Purging Room merely provides the conditions for what is already possible." He moved closer, standing beside Dion, creating a visible harmony—youth and age, spontaneity and wisdom, beginning and culmination.

"What you take from this experience is entirely your choice," Mircea continued. "As I've said, some leave and immediately begin reconstructing the same cages they temporarily escaped. Others recognize that freedom isn't found in a special room but in a quality of attention brought to every moment."

Discerning the truth of these words, the temptation to treat what Phoenix had experienced as exceptional, as separate from "real life", was already emerging. Yet a deeper part of him recognized that such compartmentalization would merely recreate the fragmentation he had begun to heal.

"Asolo seems like another lifetime," Phoenix said, recalling their first meeting in that Italian garden, the cigar shared under stars, the conversation that had planted seeds only now beginning to flower.

"Time is more mysterious than we acknowledge," Mircea replied, a knowing smile touching the corners of his mouth. "What appears linear from one perspective reveals itself as circular from another. Endings fold into beginnings. Separations prepare the ground for reunions."

His hand moved, lightly resting on Phoenix's head—a touch of blessing and recognition. "You carry the Purging Room with you now," he said softly. "Not as memory but as possibility—the possibility of bringing that same quality of mindfulness to every place you enter, every relationship you engage, every moment you inhabit." Removing his hand, he stepped back to join Dion.

The truth of this statement sounded throughout Phoenix's awareness. What he had experienced wasn't confined to this phenomenal room but available in the ordinary miracle of existence itself—if only he had eyes to see, ears to hear, and a body willing to feel.

"Thank you," he said, knowing the inadequacy of the words yet offering them anyway. "For this oasis. For the synchronicity that led me here."

"Synchronicity," Mircea's face beamed with pleasure, pleased with Phoenix's choice of words. "Yes. Not mere coincidence but meaningful connection—the universe revealing its hidden congruence to those paying attention."

His penetrating eyes held Phoenix's with gentleness. "Continue paying attention, Phoenix. The messages don't stop when you leave this room, but they do require more discernment to recognize."

Dion, watching this exchange with quiet appreciation, now stepped forward. Where Mircea carried the gravity of accumulated wisdom, Dion embodied the lightness of spontaneous identity—two essential aspects of the same mystery.

"Before you go," Dion said, with that lyrical quality Phoenix had come to associate with moments of significance in the Purging Room, "remember that wholeness isn't reached through denial of any aspect of yourself but through their harmonious expression."

He moved closer, entering Phoenix's personal space without hesitation or presumption. "The body speaks truths the mind often forgets," he said softly, echoing Mircea and O'Donohue's different expressions.

Dion bent nearer and kissed Phoenix with the same fluid grace that characterized his every moment. The contact was gentle and intentional—lips touching lips with a pressure that was neither tentative nor demanding but perfectly calibrated to the moment.

Phoenix felt a jolt penetrate his core. His first reaction was to stiffen, his breath catching in his throat. Decades of conditioning screamed in protest—this wasn't supposed to happen, and he wasn't supposed to feel anything.

His mind raced to categorize the experience, yet his body betrayed him with its honest response—warmth spreading through his extremities, his pulse quickening. The internal conflict was visceral—his body tensing while his face flushed with heat.

Part of Phoenix wanted to step back, to retreat to familiar categories and comfortable denials. But another part, perhaps the most genuine, recognized this moment as essential to his journey toward wholeness. In Dion's kiss, there was an invitation to acknowledge the full spectrum of human experience without shame or segregation.

Seconds stretched as opposing forces battled. Then, gradually, the rigidity in his posture began to soften. Not into full acceptance—he wasn't there yet—but into a willingness to exist in the question rather than rush to a comfortable answer.

The kiss lasted only seconds but contained an eternity of permission—permission to feel, to respond, to recognize aspects of his desires that his religious upbringing had deemed unacceptable, that his cultural conditioning had labeled as threatening to his identity as a man, a husband, a leader.

When Dion stepped back, pheromones lingering, his eyes held no demand for a response, no expectation of reciprocation—only a calm acknowledgment of what had been shared.

Phoenix raised his fingers and touched his lips, not in shock or shame but in wonder, in recognition. "Oh," he said softly, the sound more exhalation than word.

Dion beamed, the expression lighting his features with a beauty that existed in that ideal where opposites dissolve into unity. "Yes," he said. "Oh."

In that single syllable, Phoenix heard the echo of his experience with Pauline—the discovery of pleasure without shame. He heard Beatrix's encouragement to be more curious. He heard Silvan's guidance to recognize emotions as information instead of threats. He heard John's blessing of the body as spirit, not profane.

"Wholeness," Mircea observed quietly, his expression gentle encouragement, "requires the courage to acknowledge all aspects of your identity—including those desires your culture has taught you to fear or deny." He made a small flourish, encompassing the entire room. "Nothing truly human is foreign to the spirit."

Phoenix observed a sense of homecoming, of recognition, pieces of himself long separated, finally allowed to touch. The kiss awakened desire in his body and every aspect of himself—a quality of consciousness that was inclusive, not exclusive, embraced instead of rejected.

"It's time," Mircea said gently, indicating the door with a slight nod.

Taking a deep breath, Phoenix gathered himself for this threshold crossing. He looked again at Dion, whose face held passion and a hint of sensuality, and then Mircea, whose ardent eyes reflected understanding beyond words.

"What happens now?" he asked as they approached the doorway. One hand rested on the carved walnut surface, feeling its grain beneath his fingers. "I feel different but not wholly transformed. I am more aware of questions than answers."

"As you should be," Mircea replied. The tailored suit he wore seemed to absorb and emit light simultaneously, an impossible fabric. "True change is not a sudden replacement of one fixed state with another. It is the beginning of movement where there was stagnation, the awakening of mindfulness where there was numbness."

"So what shall I do with all of this?" His arm swept horizontally, encompassing the room and his experiences within it. The movement stirred the air of the circular room, which carried fragments of jasmine, earth, leather, and ancient paper.

"You pay attention," Mircea said. Each word carried the weight of centuries, spoken by one who had witnessed empires rise and fall. "You notice when old patterns assert themselves."

The constellation above rearranged into a new configuration, echoing Mircea's words.

"You create small spaces for new possibilities." Mircea's voice took on a musical quality. "You treat yourself with a friend's compassion rather than a critic's judgment. Gradually, almost imperceptibly, the river changes course."

A sense of permission washed through Phoenix—permission to be imperfect in the journey. He nodded slowly, understanding blooming. "Not a destination, then, a direction."

"Exactly," Mircea's smile transformed his austere features, bringing warmth to his ageless eyes. "And you have only just begun to turn toward it."

As Phoenix prepared to cross the threshold and leave the Purging Room, Mircea raised his hand in a gentle motion of pause. The silver-eyed man exchanged a meaningful glance with Dion, who nodded.

"Before you depart," Mircea said, his baritone voice carrying warmth and solemnity, "there is one final threshold to cross—the one between experience and memory."

Dion approached, carrying *The Purging Room* book with ceremonial reverence.

"What happens in this room," Mircea continued, "exists in a space between ordinary moments. Many who experience transformation here find that upon returning to their everyday world, the clarity they discovered begins to fade, like a graphic dream that dissolves with morning light."

Dion opened the book, revealing pages filled with the elegant script recording every moment of Phoenix's journey. The ink seemed to shimmer with a vitality that suggested the words were still alive, still breathing with the truth of what had transpired.

"This is why we offer you this chronicle," Mircea said as Dion extended the open book toward Phoenix. "Not merely as a record, but as a living testament to what you have experienced and who you have begun to become."

Phoenix reached for the book, feeling its substantial weight as it passed from Dion's hands to his own. As his fingers made contact with the pages, a tremor passed through him, as if the book's contents were merging with something deep-rooted within his consciousness, recognizing itself.

"When doubts arise, as they inevitably will," Mircea said, "when old patterns attempt to reassert themselves, when the world tries to convince you that transformation is impossible—open these pages. They will remind you not only of what happened here, but of what is possible."

Dion stepped nearer, placing his hand briefly atop the book while Phoenix held it. "This book will continue to write itself," he explained, his voice musical and rich. "Each choice you make, each threshold you cross, each integration you achieve or resist—all will be recorded here."

Phoenix opened it and looked down at the pages, seeing the present moment described as it unfolded, the words appearing just moments after the experience itself:

*"Phoenix opened it and looked down at the pages, seeing the present moment described as it unfolded, the words appearing just moments after the experience itself..."*

He closed the book carefully, feeling its warmth against his chest as he held it close. "Thank you," he said, the simple words inadequate for the enormity of the gift.

Mircea smiled, those silver eyes reflecting Phoenix's image back to himself—but it was a self different from the one who had entered hours before, more integrated, more aware, more alive.

"The greatest thanks," Mircea replied, "will be how you live what you have learned. The book merely reminds you of what you already know, deep within."

Dion stepped back, his graceful form creating space for Phoenix's departure. "The threshold awaits," he said softly. "As do all the pages yet to be written."

Phoenix tucked the book securely under his arm, feeling its presence like a touchstone connecting the surreal reality of the Purging Room to the ordinary world that awaited beyond the threshold. Whatever came next, this tangible artifact would remain.

"Until we meet again," Phoenix said, the phrase emerging as recognition of a pattern now set in action, a connection established that transcended the ordinary.

"Until then," Mircea agreed, inclining his head, "may you walk in freedom."

They crossed the doorway of the inner sanctum and walked along the corridor to the outer threshold. Dion moved to open the door, revealing a swirling mist that seemed to contain fragments of radiance, color, and possibility. He stood aside, making way for Phoenix to pass. Dion's expression was one of serene confidence in what awaited beyond.

oooo

Stepping onward, Phoenix crossed the threshold with the measured pace of one fully attentive to the moment's significance. The mist enveloped him, not cold or damp as he might have expected, but cozy and somehow nourishing, like being held in a gentle embrace. For a timeless moment, he existed in this in-between state—neither here nor there, neither arriving nor departing.

The mist thinned, revealing the cobblestone street where the Town Car had dropped him earlier. The fog that had shrouded Lower Manhattan had dissipated somewhat, allowing glimpses of stars between the buildings above.

Phoenix stood momentarily, allowing his senses to reorient to the ordinary world—the distant sound of traffic, the cool night air against his skin, the solid pavement beneath his feet. Yet everything seemed transformed, not by any change in the world itself but by his altered perception of it.

Street lamps glowed with an ambiance he had never noticed before, and the texture of the brick buildings revealed histories written on each weathered surface. Even his breath, visible as vapor in the cool air, seemed miraculous—the boundary between the inner and outer world made visible.

He turned, wanting one more glimpse of the walnut door, the brick façade, and the beam of light above the entrance to the Purging Room.

There was nothing there.

Only an unbroken wall of weathered brick remained where the door had been, as if the entrance he had passed through twice this evening had never existed. Phoenix blinked, momentarily disoriented, then stepped closer, running his hand along the brick surface where the door had been. The stone looked solid and unchanged for decades.

oooo

Had he imagined it all? Had the entire experience been some hallucination brought on by jet lag, drinks, and the accumulated stress of his recent life changes? Even as the questions formed, Phoenix realized their irrelevance.

Whether the Purging Room existed in the physical world or some realm of consciousness accessible under the right conditions mattered less than what had awakened within him. The clearness in his mind, the sensations in his body, the equanimity of his soul, and the freedom in his spirit were undeniably real, their effects already rippling through his existence.

It was no surprise that the door would not remain visible. Its purpose had been fulfilled; the threshold had been crossed. What awaited him now was not return but integration—bringing what he had experienced into every aspect of his life.

He stepped back from the wall, emotion forming at the corners of his mouth.

oooo

As he returned to the more populated streets where he might find transportation to his hotel, a set of headlights swept around the corner. The black Town Car that had brought him to this location hours—or was it minutes?—earlier pulled alongside him, its engine purring softly in the quiet street.

The window lowered, revealing the same Sikh driver who had engaged him in philosophical conversation on the journey here. "Sir? Did your meeting finish already? I was about to leave."

Glancing at his watch, Phoenix was surprised that only a few minutes had passed since his arrival. Time in the Purging Room had expanded and contracted according to laws different from those governing ordinary experience. "Yes," he replied, opening the car door, "My meeting is complete."

As he settled into the leather seat, the priceless chronicle in his lap, the driver glanced at him in the rearview mirror, his eyes widening. "You look different," he observed. "More—I don't know the English word. Peaceful?"

The driver's perception touched Phoenix. "I feel different," he acknowledged. "As if I've remembered an important lesson I'd forgotten."

The driver looked as if this made perfect sense. "Where to now?" he asked.

Phoenix deliberated the question, recognizing its significance beyond the immediate need for a destination. Where to, indeed? Back to his hotel, yes, but beyond that? Back to his current life, with its successes and limitations? Or onwards into a new stage, integrated and free?

"The Plaza," he said, but the word was merely a destination, not an endpoint. His mind was already racing beyond the hotel's gilded doors—toward the conversations that now seemed inevitable: with Prudence, whose certainty had once seemed like strength but now felt like armor; with Lilith, whose questions had been lifelines he'd grasped too tentatively; with partners whose respect he'd earned but whose understanding he'd never sought.

Phoenix's thoughts turned to those whose lives he had shaped most profoundly—his daughters. The realization settled in his chest: perhaps it wasn't too late for Faith to reclaim the curiosity that once made her eyes widen at constellations, for Judith to rediscover that wildhaired moment on the mountain ridge when she'd felt closest to something beyond words.

Could he influence them not through his pronouncements or corrections but through the quiet example of a father finally living truthfully? The thought of revealing a glimpse of his transformation—not the supernatural room or its guides, but the simple, revolutionary act of acknowledging his whole self—sent contradictory currents through him: terror and exhilaration, flowing together like tributaries of the same river.

Would his daughters recognize this unfamiliar, transformed father emerging from the shelter of his performances? And in witnessing his unveiling, might they glimpse their own caged selves, waiting for permission to breathe free?

As the car pulled away from the curb, Phoenix looked again at the unbroken brick wall where the entrance had been. In the diffused glow, he could almost imagine seeing the faint outline of a door—not the physical door through which he had passed but a gateway of possibility that would remain available to him always if only he dared to recognize it.

The car turned a corner, and Janus Street disappeared from view. Phoenix carried a promise of becoming, of awareness, of a life lived not in fragmented compartments but in wholeness. The Purging Room had changed him by revealing what had been buried, waiting to be recognized and embraced.

As the Town Car navigated the nighttime streets of Manhattan, Phoenix gazed out at the city with new eyes —eyes that perceived buildings, streets, and people and the spiritual atmosphere animating it all, the beauty hidden in plain sight, the wonder available in every moment to those willing to receive it.

The emptiness of self-denial was dissipating. In its place, a boundless intention took root—encompassing all he had been, all he was becoming, and all he might yet be. Phoenix smiled. Today's truth stood infinitely closer to his essence than yesterday's shadow ever could.

Some doors, once opened, can never be closed again.

# A Note from Randy

Dear Reader, Thank you for crossing the threshold into The Purging Room and accompanying Phoenix on his transformation journey. I hope these pages offer you moments of reflection, recognition, or, better yet, a doorway.

As an independent author, I rely on readers like you to help others discover this story. If this novella resonated with you in any way, I'd be deeply grateful if you would use the QR code below and leave a brief review on Amazon. Even a sentence or two about your experience with the book can make a tremendous difference. And please tell your friends.

Your thoughts matter, and I'd be honored to hear them. With appreciation, Randy Elrod

To experience more of *The Purging Room* journey, visit randyelrod.com/thepurgingroom

# Cocktail Recipes
## Inspired by *The Purging Room*

Throughout Phoenix's journey, ritual libations served as both symbols and catalysts of transformation. Each carefully crafted cocktail marked a threshold crossing, offering flavor and embodied wisdom that transcended ordinary experience.

These recipes capture the essence of those transformative elixirs. Like the experiences they represent, these cocktails are designed to engage multiple senses—visual beauty, complex aromas, and layered flavors that unfold with each sip. They invite mindful consumption as a ritual, a momentary crossing into more attentive awareness.

Whether enjoyed alone or shared with companions, these libations offer a tangible way to experience aspects of The Purging Room's integration journey—connecting mind, body, emotion, and spirit through the ancient human practice of ceremonial drink.

## The First Threshold

*(Speakeasy welcome drink. Inspired by Dion's initial absinthe preparation)*

### Ingredients:

- 1½ oz traditional Absinthe
- ½ oz elderflower liqueur (i.e., St. Germaine)
- 4-5 oz ice-cold filtered water
- 1 sugar cube
- Lemon peel

### Preparation:

1. Place sugar cube on traditional slotted absinthe spoon over glass
2. Pour absinthe and elderflower liqueur into a crystal glass
3. Slowly drip ice-cold water over sugar cube until it dissolves
4. Watch as the louche effect creates a milky opalescence
5. Express lemon peel over the surface and discard

*Tasting notes: The traditional ritual creates a drink that's simultaneously bitter and sweet, with herbal complexity that opens up as it's consumed — much like Phoenix's initial crossing into the speakeasy.*

## The Potter Inquiry

*(Inspired by the ruby integration drink)*

### Ingredients:
- 1 oz London Dry Gin
- 1 oz Creme de Cassis
- 1 oz Lillet Blanc

- 1 oz fresh lemon juice
- Mint leaf as garnish

**Preparation:**
1. Add ingredients to shaker with ice
3. Shake vigorously
4. Double strain into a small crystal glass
5. Garnish with a single mint leaf

*Tasting notes: Bright, vibrant, and slightly tart with complex notes that continue to develop – symbolizing the awakening curiosity Beatrix Potter nurtures.*

## The Réage Revelation
*(Inspired by the amber integration drink)*

**Ingredients:**
- 2 oz Cognac (XO preferred) or Brandy
- ½ oz Drambuie
- ½ oz Tio Pepe Fino Sherry
- 3 dashes orange bitters
- 4 dashes Laphroaig Whisky or wood smoke (optional: use a smoke cloche)

**Preparation:**
1. Combine ingredients in a mixing glass with ice
2. Stir until perfectly chilled
3. Strain into a small crystal glass
4. If available, capture wood smoke in cloche over drink before serving

*Tasting notes: Warm, complex, and slightly sweet with an earthiness that lingers – embodying the physical integration Phoenix experiences with Pauline Réage.*

## The Tomkins Emotion
*(Inspired by the clear integration drink)*

**Ingredients:**
- 2 oz white rum
- ½ oz Elderflower Syrup or St. Germain
- ½ oz clear crème de violette
- 1 oz fresh lime juice
- Salt and Tajin on rim

**Preparation:**
1. Rub rim and top side of small crystal glass with lime, roll in salt and tajin
2. Combine all ingredients in a mixing glass with ice
3. Stir gently until chilled
3. Strain into a small crystal glass
4. No garnish – the drink's iridescence speaks for itself

*Tasting notes: Initially seems simple but reveals surprising complexity as you sip – perfect for representing the emotional integration Phoenix experiences with Silvan Tomkins.*

## The O'Donohue Spirit
*(Inspired by the Celtic wisdom of the final encounter)*

**Ingredients:**
- 1 ½ oz Irish Whiskey
- 1 oz Brandy
- ½ oz honey
- ½ oz Benedictine
- 1 oz. lemon juice
- 5 dashes Absinthe
- Star anise

**Preparation:**
1. Shake all ingredients except star anise with ice
2. Shake until properly chilled
3. Strain into a crystal glass
4. Float star anise on top

*Tasting notes: Spirituous yet grounding, with sweetness and an aromatic quality that enhances the experience beyond mere taste – embodying the spiritual freedom O'Donohue reveals.*

## The Full Integration
*(A final celebration cocktail representing complete transformation)*

**Ingredients:**

- ½ oz Absinthe (rinse)
- 1 oz Brandy or Cognac
- 1 oz Black Tea infused Vodka (substitute: ½ black tea and ½ oz. Vodka)
- ½ oz Calavados Brandy
- ½ oz Yellow Chartreuse
- 1 oz elderflower syrup or St. Germaine
- ½ oz blueberry syrup

**Preparation:**
1. Rinse a chilled glass with Absinthe, discarding excess
2. Combine remaining ingredients in mixing glass with ice
3. Stir until perfectly chilled
4. Strain into the absinthe-rinsed glass
5. Express lemon peel over surface and discard
6. Garnish with edible flowers and Sichuan peppers

*Tasting notes: A harmonious blend that incorporates elements from all previous drinks – representing Phoenix's complete integration of body, mind, emotions, and spirit.*

# Thanks

This book owes its existence to many voices, some present and some echoing across time.

To my Beta Readers—Dan Clark, Vanessa Cordes, Ray Hensley, Abby Lane, and Benjamin Novak—who walked through early drafts with courage and candor, thank you for seeing potential in the raw material.

I am profoundly grateful to my legendary guides—Sarah Bakewell, Anaïs Nin, Carl Jung, and Carlos Ruiz Zafón—what I would not give for time, conversation, and cocktails in the Purging Room with each of them. Their words created doorways I've spent a lifetime walking through.

My sincere appreciation extends to my landlord and the construction crew who banged, hammered, sawed, and created auditory havoc just above my head throughout the finishing chapters, edits, and rewrites of this book. Their persistent reminder that transformation rarely happens in silence became an unexpected inspiration.

And finally, to my muse:

## For My Patient Muse

In the starlit hours when sentences unfold,
You've gifted me the space to be this bold.
A writer's widow, yes, but so much more—
My anchor, my first reader, whom I adore.

While characters emerged from midnight ink
And dialogue kept me too wired to think,
You weathered all my moods with patient grace,
Held our world steady when I'd lost my place.

Ten readings you endured with careful ear,
Catching each false note, making meaning clear.
Your edit pen sharper than my foggy mind,
Your heart more generous than I deserve to find.

The Purging Room exists because you do—
My threshold crosser, my *anam cara* true.
For every surly day and absent night,
I promise you: next time, I'll get it right.

# About the Author

Randy Elrod is an artist, author, and adventurer whose path has led from rural Appalachia to Barcelona's artistic streets. With works spanning memoir (*A Renaissance Redneck in a Mega-Church Pulpit*) and self-discovery (*The Quest*), his life has been marked by creative exploration and physical challenges—including twenty-five marathons and wilderness survival in Alaskan grizzly country. *The Purging Room* is his first work of fiction, written from his home in Barcelona, where he continues his mission of empowering others to embrace their authentic selves.